TRIALS

TIN STAR K9 SERIES

JODI BURNETT

SDG PUBLISHING

To the volunteers and staff of the American Society for the Prevention of Cruelty to Animals (ASPCA) who work tirelessly to rescue, protect, and care for dogs caught up in the dark and vicious world of dog fighting.

TRIALS

PROLOGUE

Caitlyn fluttered her eyelids until she could almost focus. She wasn't sure where she was until she tried to sit up. The bright lights and blinking, beeping machines were her first clue. A crushing headache was the second. The glare from the lights sent daggers of pain into her brain. Dizzy, she eased back onto the pillow.

"What happened? Where's Colt?" she asked a man wearing green hospital scrubs.

"Let me get the doctor." The man disappeared from the room, leaving Caitlyn alone and terrified. Her tongue stuck to the roof of her mouth as her heart raced. The increased pulse screamed in her head. She gripped the sheets and closed her eyes, willing herself not to cry.

"Ms. Reed?" a deep voice floated over her, and she opened her eyes, steeling herself for whatever news was coming. The gray pallor of the doctor's skin told her whatever he had to say was bad news.

"Just tell me. What happened? Where is my husband,

Colt Branson? I want to see him." Words flew from her mouth in a flurry. Blood squeezed away from her white-knuckled fists in their death-grip on the bedding.

The doctor touched her icy hand. His skin was warm against her frigid fingers. "I'm Doctor Scott. Colt is two rooms down. He's going to be fine—just a few minor cuts. He'll be here as soon as we're done patching him up. The two of you were in a car accident. Do you remember any of that?"

Caitlyn's grip eased, relieved that Colt would soon be with her, and she tried to remember. "No." She stared up at the doctor. "An accident?" She forced her mind to search for an image, a sound, something.

"Yes. A vehicle hit you on the passenger side of your car, where you were sitting. You've sustained a serious concussion, but after studying your CAT scan and MRI, I believe if you follow the concussion protocol and take care to rest and heal, you'll be fine in a month or so."

"A month? No. I need to go back to work. I have to find my dog."

"Not for a couple of weeks, you don't." Doctor Scott handed her a paper cup filled halfway with water. "Try to sip on this. Hydration is crucial for healing. Now, to properly care for your brain, you don't want any mental strain. No reading, no back-lit screens. I don't even want you to do any challenging thinking for a short period of time. Just rest. It won't be long before you're back to your normal activity. You'll want to be sure you get plenty of rest, hydration, and excellent nutrition to help your brain heal."

"Okay. I'll follow doctor's orders." She'd been through

the concussion protocol before, but she didn't have time for those things now. Not with Renegade missing. Caitlyn didn't remember much, but she knew she had been looking for her dog. She'd tell the doctor whatever he wanted to hear. She had to get out of the hospital as soon as possible.

"Good." The ER doctor patted her hand and looked toward the door. "I'll talk with you more about your care plan as soon as your husband gets here."

Caitlyn's intuition revved into full gear. Something was off with the doctor. There was something he wasn't telling her.

A nurse wheeled Colt into her room in a chair, but the moment he was through the door, he leapt to his feet and hurried to her. He took her hands in his bandaged ones, his eyes searching hers.

"What happened to your hands?" She lifted them tenderly before stretching her fingers to his forehead. "You cut your head."

"I'm fine, Catie." He held up his bandages. "I have a few minor cuts and scrapes is all, but I'm worried about *you*." Colt swiped a long strand of her dark brown hair behind her ear. "I didn't know."

"Didn't know... what?" Caitlyn dipped her eyebrows at her husband and then swung her gaze to the doctor, who avoided her eyes. "Didn't know *what*?" she asked again, firmer, louder.

Colt's eyes darkened as they pivoted in the same direction. "You didn't tell her?"

The doctor hugged a clipboard to his chest. "I thought

it was best to wait for you, so you could be with her for support."

Caitlyn pushed herself up on the bed. Obviously, Colt and the doctor had had a conversation before now. "Tell me what? Did you learn something about Renegade?" she demanded. Her mind went fuzzy, and taking a breath, she eased back against her pillow. The tension in the room exhausted her.

Colt sat on the edge of her bed and held her hands, though it must have been painful. He met her gaze. "We lost our baby, sweetheart." Tears trembled on his lower lids, and he bowed to kiss her hands. Caitlyn went still.

"What baby? What are you talking about? Are you saying that something awful has happened to Renegade?" Searing darts flew up her spine and blasted through her skull. Memories of the previous night rushed back to her consciousness all at once. Someone had stolen Renegade from their hotel room. "Colt, what happened? Where is he?" Panic thickened the walls of her throat. "Is Renegade dead?"

Colt sat back, staring at her. He swallowed. "No, Catie. Renegade is still missing. And we'll find him. I'm talking about *our* baby. Yours and mine. You didn't tell me you were pregnant. I'm so sorry."

At a loss, Caitlyn pulled her hands away from Colt. She stared at him for a moment before she turned to the doctor. It seemed as though her head was stuffed with cotton. She heard their words, but none of it made sense. It was like coming into a movie when it was half over. "Pregnant?"

The color drained from Colt's face, and he stroked her

cheek with fingertips poking out from the gauze. "You didn't know?"

Dread from an ugly dark place deep inside welled up, and Caitlyn's head shook from side to side. She grimaced and pressed her fingertips to her temples. "No. No, you're wrong. I don't know what you're saying."

Colt pulled her into his arms, but it didn't help as her mind grappled with what he'd said. She *was* pregnant, but now she *wasn't*? Reflexively, she pushed him away.

"I'm so sorry, sweetheart." The tears that threatened earlier dripped down his cheeks. He was obviously devastated, but she still couldn't grasp the gravity of his words.

The doctor cleared his throat. "I'm admitting you to the hospital for a couple of days. I want to monitor your brain, and the obstetrician on call will want to do some tests."

"No. I can't stay here. I have to find my dog." Caitlyn wasn't about to be stuck in a hospital. She wanted to leave. She wanted to be alone, so she didn't have to think about any of this. She wanted the words Colt had said to her to evaporate. She wanted Renegade.

Colt scooted closer to her. "This is all too much right now. Let's get you to a room where you can rest. We can talk there if you want."

Caitlyn's heart raced as her breath quickened. Her head swam, and her throat constricted against a metallic taste at the back of her throat. She gagged. "I'm—"

Seeing what was happening, the doctor grabbed a plastic basin just in time. Caitlyn threw up, heaving several times before she dissolved into tears. Colt held her shoulders until she finished and then he wiped her mouth and nose with a tissue. Saying nothing, he pulled her into his arms, where she fell apart.

Everything crashed into her mind and heart at once. She had wondered why she was so tired all the time. She was pregnant. But now she wasn't. She'd lost a little one she didn't even know she'd had. Pain threatened to crush her chest, her head. Her throat ached with sorrow.

And she hadn't only lost their baby. She'd lost her best friend. The only way she'd survive this was if she found him. After she spent her tears, Colt held a cup of water to her lips. He kissed her forehead.

"We'll get through this together," he murmured against her skin.

She was numb. His words should have brought her comfort, but she had no feeling at all. "I want to leave the hospital. We must find Renegade." Caitlyn had to focus on finding her dog. It was the only way she would survive the loss of their baby.

1
___

The ER doctor admitted Caitlyn to the hospital, though she did not want to stay. "Colt, please. We're wasting time, and minutes are crucial in a kid... dog-napping case."

"Your health is the most important thing, Catie. What good will you be to Renegade if you don't take care of yourself? Please, listen to the doctors."

"I don't even know these doctors. And I certainly don't trust them." Caitlyn allowed anger to swell inside her chest. It was a much more powerful emotion than sorrow. Anger helped her feel more in control. Fear and grief threatened to knock her off her feet. She couldn't let that happen, so she chose anger instead.

A nurse wheeled Caitlyn's hospital bed from the ER into an empty room in the medical wing. "Here we are. I'll get you all hooked up before Doctor Whitman comes in."

"Who is Doctor Whitman?" Caitlyn looked at her wrist for the time. "Where is my watch?"

Colt took her hand. "I have it. Don't worry."

"Don't worry? Come on, Colt. I can't do anything in this place but worry."

The nurse finished attaching Caitlyn to the machines and refreshed her IV. She held up the remote control. "This is for your bed and the TV. Of course, in your case, no TV. You can also call me from here if you need anything. Okay?"

"Yes—fine," Caitlyn grumbled. She wanted the woman to leave the room.

Still holding her hand, Colt sat on the edge of her bed. He brought her fingers to his lips. "It was a long night. You should probably try to get some sleep." He shifted his gaze to the window. His Adam's apple slid up and down his neck. "Unless you want to talk."

His words raised an intense emotion she wanted to stuff deep down, and she pulled her hand away. "What I want is to get out of here and find Renegade. Don't you?" She glared at him accusingly. Anything to keep hot tears from flowing.

Colt scooted closer and brushed her cheek and twirled a long curl around his finger. Frustrated by the gauze, he unwound the bandaging on his hands and threw it away. The cuts he had were relatively minor and would heal quickly. "Of course, I want to find him. But right now, I'm more concerned about you. The cops are on the case. It isn't like no one is doing anything."

"Are they investigating the hit-and-run, too?"

"Yes. Especially since we lost..." He swallowed again, "The baby. The police consider the hit and run a manslaughter case."

Caitlyn squeezed her eyes shut and gripped her fingers into tight fists, terrified of losing control.

"Hey, come here." Colt pulled her into his arms and held her head against his chest. "It's okay to let go. I'm here. I've got you."

His kindness and strength were too much for her to battle, and her body shuddered with a great sob. Then the tears flooded her eyes and cheeks. She nuzzled deeper into Colt's embrace and let them come. When they did, she was certain they'd never stop. Colt shifted their bodies and lay next to her, holding her tight while her grief engulfed her. He murmured loving, comforting sounds into her hair, but she couldn't focus on the words. It was enough to know he was there for her.

Footfalls sounded on the tile floor, and Colt pushed himself up on his elbow. A soft, feminine voice apologized. "Excuse me. Sorry to intrude. I'm Doctor Whitman the OBGYN on call. I'll come back in a few minutes."

Caitlyn didn't bother to open her eyes and let Colt handle the woman. "Thank you," his deep tone vibrated against her temple. The doctor left the room and Colt kissed Caitlyn's forehead. "Here's a tissue. I'll get you some water." He got off the bed, and her whole body missed him.

She dabbed at her damp face and pushed herself up on the bed to sip the ice water Colt handed her. "Thanks, that helps."

"Are you ready to talk to the doctor?"

Caitlyn released a sigh that made her chest ache. "I guess."

Colt opened the door and gestured for Doctor Whitman to come in.

"Hi Caitlyn, I hear you had an awful night."

The last thing Caitlyn wanted to do was talk about all that had happened. "What time is it?"

Colt glanced at his watch. "Ten-fifteen."

Doctor Whitman nodded as she read from her file. "I'd like to discuss the D&C procedure you need, and then you should try to get some sleep. Have you had anything to eat?"

"No. And I'm not having any procedure."

The doctor raised her eyes to meet Caitlyn's. She darted her gaze to Colt and rested it once again on Caitlyn. "Do you have concerns about having a D&C?"

"I don't see the purpose, and I'm not one to go through unnecessary medical treatments." It was difficult to talk over the swollen lump in her throat. "As you say, the pregnancy is over. I just want to get out of here and get on with things. My K9 partner is missing, and I need to help find him."

"Why don't I explain why I believe it is a wise thing to do, and then we can discuss it? How does that sound?"

"Not right now. Didn't you say I need to eat and sleep? I'll do that."

"Catie, the doctor is just trying to give you your options so you can make an informed decision," Colt lifted her hand and laced his fingers with hers.

She pulled her hand away. "Look, no offense, but I don't know you. I have my own doctor who I trust."

Doctor Whitman's face softened with a gentle smile. "I

understand. Why don't you order some food—the cafeteria is on call twenty-four-seven—and then get some rest." She jotted something down on a sticky pad. "When you're feeling a little better, call your doctor and talk about your situation." She handed Colt the note. "This is my cell number. Please have your doctor call me with any questions or concerns." She touched the covers over Caitlyn's foot. "I'll come back at the end of my day and see how you're feeling."

"Thank you." Colt walked the doctor out into the hall, no doubt apologizing for his wife's abruptness.

Caitlyn didn't care that she was direct to the point of being rude. She was desolately empty inside. Why would she let doctors scrape away anything that remained? What if they were wrong? What if they just *thought* she'd lost the baby, but she hadn't and she let them do the procedure? She shivered and pulled the blankets up to her chin.

Colt returned with a menu. "The nurse said you could order whatever you'd like from this." He handed her the laminated sheet.

Caitlyn read the options, and her stomach rumbled in anticipation. "I want mashed potatoes with gravy and a chocolate milkshake." She rested her head against the pillow.

"Want some chicken or a burger with that?"

"No, thanks. Not right now."

Her husband lifted the phone and dialed. He ordered her comfort food and a burger for himself. "You'll feel better after you eat." He pulled the visitor's chair close to the side of the bed and sat. Steepling his fingers, he rested his chin on his hands. "I think you should get another opinion about the D&C."

Caitlyn chewed on her lip. "I just want to look for Renegade."

"I know, sweetheart, but the local cops are looking for him. They're doing everything they can. Right now, you need to take care of yourself."

"I'm fine. Really. I'll take care of myself when I have Ren back." Caitlyn prayed that whoever took him was taking care of him as she resolutely pushed away darker thoughts. "I wish we never came here. All of this for a title? A little recognition that means nothing? What was I thinking?"

"Whoa." Colt took her hand in both of his. "The trials were fun, Renegade was amazing, and we met some good people. Besides, there's no way you can ever predict what's going to happen. If you try, you'll end up closing yourself up in a closet, so you don't get hurt." He kissed her fingertips. "I'm going to refill your water. Do you need anything else while I'm up?"

A young nurse in purple scrubs entered the room. "Just here to check your vitals." She looked at the machines behind the bed and wrote a few notes before swiping Caitlyn's forehead with a digital thermometer. "Okay, that's all. Sorry for interrupting."

"Thanks." Colt handed Caitlyn fresh ice water and took his seat.

"Colt..." She swallowed her fear of the possibility the fetus was still intact. He'd think she was crazy for thinking such a thing when the doctors told them the baby was gone. She knew it made no sense, but still... what if?

"What is it?" He scooted closer and stroked her leg.

She escaped having to say more when a woman wheeled in a tray carrying their food. "Here we are." She placed the food on the wheeled table and rolled it to Caitlyn's bed. "Give us a call if you need anything else."

Colt stood when she entered, and he followed her to the door, closing it behind her when she left. Returning to Caitlyn's side, his eyes softened. "Let me know if you want some of my burger. I know you've got your favorite comfort food, but you should probably have some protein, too."

"I'm fine." The buttery scent of the potatoes caused her stomach to cramp with hunger. She took a big bite of the creamy potatoes and closed her eyes. These were the real deal—not the watered-down instant kind—and the warm softness soothed her achy throat. When her belly was full, sleepiness took over, but a phone buzzed, and she opened her eyes.

"Hi, Stella." He smiled at Caitlyn. "Yeah, she just finished a big bowl of mashed potatoes and is getting ready to take a nap." Colt closed his eyes as he listened, swallowing hard. He ran a hand across his face. "She got a bad concussion, and..." His jaw bulged, and he lowered Caitlyn's phone briefly.

Stella's voice echoed from his cupped hand. "Colt? Are you there? Is Caitlyn alright? Colt?"

"Sorry, Stella." He cleared his throat and turned his back to Caitlyn. "The doctors discovered Catie was pregnant but—but she... uh... lost the baby in the collision."

Colt squeezed his eyes shut as he listened to his mother-in-law's voice, then he handed Caitlyn her phone.

She didn't want to take it, but she had to. "Hi, Mom." As soon as she heard her mother's voice, she broke into silent tears, not wanting her mom to realize the depth of her pain.

"Oh, honey, I'm so sorry to hear about the baby. I wish I was there with you right now."

Caitlyn nodded but couldn't speak. There were no words.

CAITLYN DROPPED her phone onto the bed and buried her face in her hands. She was always so tough, but the combination of her grief, the accident, and her fear for Renegade had brought her to her knees. He lifted the phone. "Stella, Catie can't talk right now. I think we're going to talk to another doctor and get more information. We'll let you know what we learn, and Catie will call you back from the phone in her room after she's had some sleep. My phone was smashed, so I'll have hers if you need to reach me."

"I understand. Oh, Colt, I'm so sorry about all of this. It's an incredibly difficult time. Please take care of her. Be gentle. You know she'll try to pretend that she can handle it, but this is a deep loss. She's going to need you now more than ever."

"I know. We'll call back after Catie has had a nap and we talk to the doctors."

"Please tell her I love her. I can come down there if you need me to."

"Thanks. I'll let her know." Colt ended the call.

Caitlyn's voice was small. "I'm sorry. I just couldn't talk right now."

Colt squeezed her hand. "She understands."

"I think I want to call Blake. At least we know him and can trust his advice."

"He's not an OBGYN, though." A vague irritation passed through Colt at Caitlyn's desire to call their town doctor. He was sure there was nothing between the two of them anymore and that they'd all moved far past the time Caitlyn was dating the flashy doctor, but it niggled at him that she wanted to turn to Blake, nonetheless.

"I know, but he'll still be able to advise me."

A knock sounded on the door, and the face of Officer Berkley, the K9 cop who had leant them his specialized vehicle while they were in Arizona, peeked through the opening. "Hey, I'm sure you don't want visitors right now, but my wife sent a care package with some things, like a toothbrush and some other stuff you might need. And I have a little information on the hit and run case."

Caitlyn seemed to shrink into the bed, but she waved for Officer Berkley to enter. "What did you find out?"

He set a basket with basic toiletry items on the bedside table and jammed his hands into his pockets. "We pulled some paint chips from the creases in the side of my vehicle. They're at the lab now."

"That's a long shot." Colt dragged a second chair next to his, and they both sat.

"It is, but it could tell us the manufacturer and the

year of the vehicle that hit you. Then we'll check around with all the body shops and junk yards to see if they've had anyone with that criteria come in. By the level of impact, we believe it was a truck that hit you."

Caitlyn pushed herself up and cleared her throat. "What have you found out about Renegade? Do you have anything?"

"No, nothing, yet. But all units on the road are looking for him."

A single tear trickled down Caitlyn's cheek, and it cut through Colt's heart. He felt utterly helpless. He had to go out and search for Renegade. If they could find him, Caitlyn's dog would be the best medicine for her grief. But he didn't want to leave her alone at the hospital.

Caitlyn brushed at her damp cheek. "I have to get out of here. I want to help look for him."

"Catie," a pure jolt of anguish shot through his chest. "You can't leave the hospital. You have to rest. I'll meet up with Berkley and help them with the search later, after you have a nap."

Officer Berkley's phone rang, and he stood to answer it, walking to the far corner of the room. When he returned, he said, "The paint from the accident reveals that it was definitely a Ford that broadsided you. It was either a truck or a Bronco from 1994 through 1997. The paint color is called Indigo Blue Metallic."

A beam of hope had Colt on his feet. "That narrows it down. We have to find that vehicle."

2

———

Colt's eyes flew to Caitlyn, who sat straight up on the bed. "Colt, go help them. There's no point in you sitting here when you could be looking for Ren. Please, go. Find my dog."

He swallowed, unsure of the best decision, but Caitlyn was clear about what she wanted. "Mind if I ride into the office with you, Officer Berkley? I want to help with the investigation in any way I can."

"Sure, and call me Dan. We're mostly making phone calls at this point. Hopefully, the hit-and-run driver took his vehicle to a body shop somewhere in town."

"Thanks. Yeah, that would make it easy. If you'll just give us a minute, I'll be right out."

After Officer Berkley left the room, Colt took a seat on the edge of Caitlyn's bed. "Promise me you'll take a nap while I'm gone. When I return, we can decide about the procedure."

Uncharacteristically, Caitlyn seemed to draw back. She shook her head and stared at her clasped hands resting on the sheet. Her voice faltered. "I don't want to do it, Colt. I'm afraid."

"What are you afraid of?" He covered her hands with one of his. Her fingers were unusually cold.

Her deep brown eyes searched his as they grew damp. "I know this sounds crazy, but what if I didn't actually lose the baby? What if I was just bleeding a little, and the baby is still inside? If I let them do the D&C..."

A sharp pain darted through Colt's chest, and he gathered his wife into his arms. "I'm sure that's not the case, sweetheart. But let's talk to the doctor about it, so you can be certain."

"But I don't know this doctor. How can I trust her?"

"Okay, let's call Blake, then, if you think that will help."

"It might, but he'll probably think I'm being ridiculous."

"No, he won't. Hell, he's still in love with you. He would never think you were ridiculous."

The tiny smile he'd hoped for twitched at the side of Caitlyn's mouth. "He is *not*." She shoved his arm, sending relief through him like warm whiskey. It wasn't like Caitlyn to be tentative or afraid and Colt prayed Blake Kennedy could help her. The doctor *was* still in love with Colt's wife, no matter what Caitlyn believed. Blake had feelings for her left over from the short time they dated before Colt and Caitlyn got together. But they had all become friends over time and hopefully Blake could comfort her now.

Colt pressed the number for Blake on Caitlyn's phone and set the call on speaker.

"Well, hello, Caitlyn. I'm surprised to hear from you. I heard you and Colt were out of town."

"We are," Colt answered, letting the doctor know he was on the line too. We're in Scottsdale, and you're on speaker. Listen Blake, Caitlyn is in the hospital."

"Why? What happened?" The deep concern filling Blake's voice rubbed against Colt's nerves.

"There is a long version, but the short story is we were in a car accident last night and Catie is in the hospital. She's right here with me."

"Caitlyn?"

"Hi, Blake. I'm here. I'm okay, except for a concussion."

"There's more to it than that if they admitted you to the hospital. What's the name of your doctor?"

"There's more," Colt continued. "Her doctor's name is Whitman. She's an OBGYN."

"Okay..."

Colt took a shallow breath and swallowed, avoiding the pain in Caitlyn's eyes. "We didn't know it before, but the doctors told us that Catie was pregnant. They say she lost the baby in the collision."

Blake was silent for several uncomfortable seconds. "I'm very sorry to hear that. Caitlyn, how are you feeling?"

Tears filled her eyes and, covering her mouth with her fingers, she shook her head.

"She has a headache and is tired, but we called you because she's worried. The doctor wants to do something called a D&C, but Catie's not sure she should have it done."

"Caitlyn? I wish I was there so I could see your face. You've suffered a tremendous shock, and I'm sure your emotions are confused."

She wiped her eyes with the back of her hand and sniffed. "Yeah."

"Did Doctor Whitman explain the procedure and the reason for it?"

"I know what it is."

"Colt? How about you?"

"I don't know much. Just that the doctor thinks it's necessary."

"Basically, a D&C, or dilation and curettage, is a procedure where they open the cervix and insert a thin instrument into the uterus, which is used to remove any remaining tissue and clear the uterine lining. They do this to prevent continual bleeding and the possibility of infection."

Colt perched his hands on his hips. All of this was beyond his experience and knowledge. "So, you would recommend Catie have it done?"

Blake neglected to answer Colt's question. "Caitlyn, what are your concerns?"

Her cheeks went pink when she glanced up at Colt, and she chewed on her lower lip before she answered Blake's question. "You'll think I'm being foolish."

"There are no foolish questions. It's your body. Ask any questions you have."

"I was just worried that... well... what if the doctors are wrong? What if the accident caused me to bleed, but the baby is still there? Is that possible?"

"Ah. I understand why you're feeling hesitant. I'm

truly sorry to say that is highly unlikely. There are tests, like an ultrasound and blood tests, to measure hCG, which is a hormone produced by the placenta. Did they do these tests?"

"Catie was unconscious when she got to the ER, and they took me to a different exam room to clean out some cuts on my hands. I'm not sure if they did them or not."

Caitlyn gave her chewed-on lip a break to answer. "Doctor Whitman came in to talk with me, but it wasn't a good time. She said she'd come back."

"Okay, I'll call her at the hospital and double check, but Caitlyn, they wouldn't say you miscarried if they didn't know for certain. I'll inform Whitman that you and I would like to see all test results, so we can be sure before you make any decisions. There are other options, but honestly, I would make the same recommendation as the doctor there. It is a quick procedure, and you should be back on your feet tomorrow. But you'll want to take it easy for a couple of days."

Colt chuffed. "You do know who you're talking to, right?"

"I do, but I'm serious, Caitlyn. You *need* to rest. Your body has gone through a lot in the past twenty-four hours."

While Colt ended the call with Kennedy, his wife hugged her knees up to her chin and rested her forehead on them. He set her phone face down on the bedside table. "Did it help to talk to Blake?"

"Sort of. I mean, I understand all that he said, but I had a tiny hope that maybe..." The tears returned.

Colt's chest pressed against the swelling ache growing

inside. He was helpless to fix this for Caitlyn—helpless to ease her pain. "I'll stay with you until you fall asleep, then I'm going to the police department to see if they've learned anything about Renegade or if they've found the vehicle that hit us. I'll be back by the time Doctor Whitman returns. How does that sound?"

Caitlyn released a long sigh that must have come from her toes. "You don't have to stay till I fall asleep. Officer Berkley is out in the hall waiting for you, and I'll be fine. But please, Colt, you must find Renegade."

3

—————

Blake set his phone back in the cradle and, gripping the edge of his desk, he closed his eyes. Raw jealousy coursed through him at the thought of Caitlyn carrying Colt's baby. The desire to rush down to Scottsdale to hold her hand and protect her was strong, and he had to wrestle it back.

He took several deep breaths before looking up Doctor Whitman. The search revealed that the OBGYN had an excellent reputation, which helped ease some of his jumbled emotions and his need to be with Caitlyn through all she was dealing with. He murmured out loud to himself. "She's married, asshole. Move on."

He picked up his cell phone and called the number of a woman he'd met in Spearfish a couple of weeks prior. They'd had dinner twice since then. Coincidentally, she lived in Moose Creek too, but even so, Blake took her to restaurants outside the little town. He loved Moose Creek, except when he wanted to be discrete. The last thing he wanted to do was feed the gossip mill in their tiny burg, especially when he didn't know if there was a future for their new relationship. He liked his privacy and there was no such thing in their close-knit community.

"Well, hello," her silky voice slid around him. "I wondered when I'd hear from you."

"Hey. Do you have any plans tonight?"

"Depends. What do you have in mind?"

Blake took a deep breath and let it out slowly. "I was thinking I might cook dinner for you at my place."

"Well, now. That sounds cozy. Let me check on some arrangements. Can I let you know?"

"Sure. I just need a little time to get groceries."

"I'll call you right back." She released a sexy little giggle, and Blake focused on the promise of the sound.

After Caitlyn ended things between them, he rebounded with a woman who ended up becoming his fiancé. But that didn't last, and he had dated no one since Kayla left him. Blake didn't blame his ex for leaving. She was right when she claimed he was still hung up on Caitlyn. But he had loved Kayla too, and he believed they could have had an enjoyable life together. After all, Caitlyn was the first woman he'd ever truly loved, and he would always carry her in his heart. But she was married to Colt now, and that was that. The issue with Kayla was she had wanted every ounce of Blake to herself. And he would have given it to her—if he could have.

Blake still lived in the house he'd bought for Kayla and himself on the golf course. The rear of the custom-built home looked out on the seventeenth hole. It had been a warm autumn, but it was too cold to have a romantic dinner on the deck, so he'd light some candles. The view would still impress.

He listened to his messages at the end of the day. Doctor Whitman had emailed him Caitlyn's medical files, confirming the necessity of her D&C. He wished he could be in Arizona with Caitlyn. He told himself it was because he wanted to reassure her, but there was more to it than that. He gave the files a quick scan to confirm what he already thought was true and then called Caitlyn's hospital room.

"Hey, how are you doing?"

"Okay." Caitlyn sounded exhausted.

"Getting some rest?"

"I'm trying. Did you have a chance to look at my test results?"

"I have, and I agree with your doctor there. I would also advise you to have the procedure. And I'm sorry for what you're going through."

Caitlyn's breath sounded ragged over the phone before she answered. "Okay. I trust you."

"Call me after. I want to know how you're feeling. Okay."

"Yeah. Thanks, Blake." She ended the call.

Blake sighed and moved on to his next phone message, receiving confirmation of his dinner plans. He texted his date the address and went to find his Porsche in the clinic parking lot.

The days of driving his sports car were coming to an end due to the pending autumn weather. They could get snow in Wyoming any day. Blake laughed at himself as he revved the powerful engine, remembering how he'd arrived in the mountain town with only the sleek Porsche to drive. Since then, he'd wised up and got himself a shiny red Range Rover Sport for winter driving.

Good thing it was still warm enough to grill outside. Steaks were the only thing he really knew how to cook. When he got home with the groceries, he noticed his cleaner had come through. Perfect, clean bathrooms and fresh sheets.

An hour later, his doorbell rang. He opened it to a hot blonde whose bright red lips curled into a seductive smile. "Hello, handsome."

"Hello, yourself. Come on in." He stood to the side and appreciated her figure as she passed by. "Let me take your coat." He breathed in her spicy perfume as he slid her wrap from her shoulders. "Can I get you a glass of wine?"

"Yes, thanks. The room looks amazing with all these candles," she ran her scarlet tipped fingernails along the back of the couch as she walked by. "Nice house."

This woman was as different from Caitlyn as he could imagine. She was the type he was used to from when he lived in the city. Glossy and sexy as hell. He poured her a glass of Cabernet, and coming up behind her, he reached around to hand her the glass, dropping several kisses along her neck.

"Feeling a little frisky tonight?" She took the glass and turned to face him, blinking her big blue eyes at him.

Frisky wasn't the right term. He was desperate. He needed to lose himself in this woman so that he could evict Caitlyn from his mind. "Hungry?" He smiled.

"Those dimples are adorable." She touched his cheek and stretched up to kiss him.

She tasted like honey, and he gathered her in his arms. The feelings she stirred were sure to do the trick, but he was a gentleman. He pulled away from her. "I have stuffed mushrooms for an appetizer. Have a seat, and I'll be right back."

With a cute little pout, she swayed to the picture window. "This is a gorgeous view. How long have you lived here?"

"Almost a year." He poured himself a glass of wine and brought the plate of re-heated mushrooms to the coffee table. "It's handy for when I want to get in a round of golf."

"I can imagine." She nibbled on a mushroom. "Make these yourself?" She grinned as she popped the rest of it into her mouth.

"Hey, now. Be nice. I'm a doctor, not a chef." He reached across and wiped a crumb from her lip.

"I'm not complaining. They're good. Besides, I'm impressed that you pulled all of this together after your day at work. Thanks for inviting me." Her gaze appreciatively panned the open floor plan of his custom timber home. As she looked around, he saw his space through new eyes. The square beams with their black cleats and heavy bolts suited him, and the view was one of which he'd never tire.

Blake hadn't brought a woman home since Kayla left. But it was time. Besides, he wanted to spend more time with this beauty and needed a place where there were no speculative eyes watching their every move.

After they shared most of the appetizer, Blake took the seasoned rib-eyes out to the grill. "I hope you're hungry."

"More than you know." Her smooth voice caressed his skin, sending a thrilling zing through his body.

Dinner was going well until Blake went to get the cheesecake he'd bought for dessert. He scooped a bite from his fork and held it for her to taste. But instead of taking it, she asked, "Did I hear you used to date Caitlyn Reed?"

He almost dropped the fork, and he jerked his chin back in surprise. "Yeah, we dated a short time. Where did you hear that from?"

"Oh, around. It doesn't matter to me. I was just curious. She seems to get around."

Blake wasn't sure what she meant by that. "Not really. She's married now, anyway."

"Yes. Too bad. I mean, she left you for the man she married, right?"

Blake took a long drink of his wine. "Where's this going?" She shrugged it off. Which was good because he definitely didn't want to talk about Caitlyn, especially with a woman he was hoping to spend the night with. "I can't stand the gossip in this town. I hope you don't mind if we keep our... friendship just between the two of us for a while."

"I don't mind. I think it's kind of fun. Romantic. I just wanted to know if you're seeing anyone else. You know, trying to figure out where I stand."

He could honestly encourage her there. "There's no one besides you."

She wrapped her plump lips around the bite of dessert and pulled it from his fork. Her eyes closed briefly in pleasure, which made his mind jump to the bedroom. "Good. That's exactly what I wanted to hear." She slid from her chair onto his lap. "How about we save the cheesecake 'til after dessert?"

4

———

Since his phone was crushed in the accident, Colt took Caitlyn's cell with him. It rang as he rushed through the hospital corridors to meet Dan Berkley at his squad car in front of the hospital. It was Dylan—*shit*—he had forgotten to call Caitlyn's brother. Colt should have called the family with an update, but so much was going on and he was barely holding on. He had no control over any of it and that left him feeling wrung out.

"Hey, Dylan. Sorry I haven't gotten back to you. Caitlyn is awake and doing pretty good. She has a severe concussion."

"Thank, God that's all. We were worried."

"I know. I'm sorry. We were dealing with some... stuff."

"What *stuff*?" Irritated suspicion rang through Dylan's tone. He was ever Caitlyn's older and extremely protective brother. That would never change.

Colt's throat swelled with sudden emotion. How did

you tell someone you lost a baby you didn't know you had? "We, uh... apparently, Catie was pregnant. We didn't know."

"What do you mean by *was*?"

A rock formed against his tonsils, and Colt couldn't answer. The heavy mantle of failure draped over his shoulders. He should have been able to protect his wife and child somehow. It was his first test at fatherhood, and he had failed.

Dylan's voice dropped. "Did she lose the baby in the accident?"

"Yeah." The word squeezed painfully out on a groan.

"I'm sorry, man. Is Caitlyn okay?"

"Not really. She's sad and scared. We talked to Blake earlier. I think that helped her a little." Colt wished he could take her pain away, but as it was, he prayed she wouldn't withdraw from him. His wife was a proud woman and didn't have patience with emotions she thought made her weak.

"And Renegade? Any news?"

"No. I've got to find him. He's the one thing that will bring Catie comfort. God, Dylan. I feel so damn helpless."

"You probably feel a lot more than that. I know how devastated I was when Wendy Gessler was killed, and along with her, our baby. There was no one for me to talk to at the time, but you've got me... if you need a shoulder."

Wendy Gessler's murder was what brought Colt and Caitlyn together again after years of not speaking. Caitlyn was determined to prove that Dylan was not the killer, and Bruce Tackett, the Moose Creek sheriff at the time, was equally invested in proving that Dylan was. Colt had been a deputy back then and was in on the investigation. It was during that case that Caitlyn realized she wanted to be in law enforcement. And they both realized they still loved each other. Colt had almost forgotten there was a baby in the middle of the whole mess.

"Thanks, Dyl. I'm just trying to understand why I'm so shattered by this when I didn't even know the little person existed until last night."

"Caitlyn didn't tell you?"

"She didn't know either. And I've never seen her so upset. First, with Renegade missing and then the miscarriage on top of that."

"What's your plan?"

"I'm on my way to the police department to assist with the accident investigation and to help them search for Renegade. I have to do something. Caitlyn is staying overnight in the hospital. She's supposed to be sleeping, but I doubt she is."

"Text me the hospital she's in and her room number. I'll give her a call there. I wish I was down there with you guys."

"Talking to you will mean a lot to her, I'm sure. And Dylan—thanks. I feel your support. It helps to know you understand what I'm going through."

"Yeah, helpless as hell and completely devastated. But I'm here for you, man, if you need me. Hang in there."

Colt ended the call and waved to Berkley through the glass door.

At the Scottsdale Police Department Headquarters,

Colt followed Dan through an office maze to the desks of the two detectives assigned to their case.

"Detectives, this is Sheriff Branson from Wyoming. He and his wife were the victims of that hit and run last night. Sheriff, these are Detectives Webb and Albrecht."

The senior detective of the two, Darin Webb, a tall, skinny man whose crumpled paper-bag of a suit was two sizes too big, sat on the edge of his desk. His close-cropped dark hair harkened back to a bygone era from half a century ago. "Happy to help fellow law enforcement officers." Webb shook Colt's hand. "Did Berkley tell you about the paint chips we found on the vehicle you and your wife were in?"

"Yeah. He said they were Indigo Blue Metallic—belonging to a Ford Bronco or truck."

"And there were no skid marks at the scene. Which means the driver of the Ford didn't try to slam on his breaks to avoid the collision."

"Maybe the driver was drunk and didn't see us. Has there been any luck locating the missing vehicle, or K9 Renegade?" He hoped using Ren's K9 designation would help spur urgency in the detectives.

"Not so far." Webb's partner, Detective J.D. Albrecht, a compact man in his forties, with light brown hair and a graying goatee, answered, "We have our day shift officers canvassing the area around the accident and your hotel. They're looking for eyewitnesses or video feeds from security cameras on the local businesses. But nothing, yet."

Colt clenched his teeth together and rested his hands on his hips where his utility belt and gun usually were.

He knew they were doing the best they could, but he wanted them to do more and do it faster.

He sighed. "Sounds like you're doing what you can about the accident, but honestly, the greater concern is the dog. Think of his abduction in the same way you would if someone took your partner. Whatever lengths you would go to find him, we need to use those same efforts to rescue Renegade. Have you talked to anyone from Animal Control?"

Albrecht shook his head. "The dognapping is a separate investigation, and it is being handled by them. Let me get their number."

A phone on the desk rang and Webb answered it, turning his back to the rest of them. He pressed his free ear closed with his fingertips while he spoke. Finally, he spun around and tossed the receiver into its cradle like a mic-drop. "Good news. One of our officers got hold of a video from an ATM across the street from your hotel."

"That's great!" Colt's heart flew to his throat. "Can they see who took Renegade?"

"No. Unfortunately, the view doesn't encompass your room; it only shows the hotel entrance. But it recorded a light blue, late-model Ford truck idling in the parking lot. The video isn't clear enough to make out the identity of the driver, but when the truck pulls away, you can clearly see two digits and a letter on an Arizona license plate."

Albrecht rubbed his hands together. "It's only a matter of time now. We'll get the computer searching for that license plate, and soon we'll know who the truck is registered to."

Colt crunched his eyebrows together. "Wait. So, the truck that hit us was at our hotel?"

"We can't be certain it's the same truck, but it would sure be a tremendous coincidence if it wasn't." Webb turned his computer monitor to face them and clicked open the email with the video feed attached. He played the tape. "Don't you think? I mean, how many '90s trucks do you see driving around anymore?"

Colt stared at the monitor and sweat trickled down his spine. He rubbed his back to get rid of the tickle. "What's the time stamp on this feed?"

"5:42 pm on the evening of the accident," Albrecht read.

"They must have been casing our room!" Queasiness gripped Colt by the throat. "Does this mean the wreck wasn't an accident? Could they have followed us and tried to..." He had to sit down. "My wife could have been killed."

"Yep, it's starting to look like it was intentional. Is there anyone in Phoenix who has a grudge against you two? Anyone who'd want to do you or your wife harm?"

"No. We don't know anybody down here at all."

A female uniformed cop approached the detective's desk carrying a large manila envelope with a cowboy hat resting on top of it. She gave Colt a curt nod. "Are you Sheriff Branson?"

"I am."

"I have you and your wife's personal items from the car accident last night. Lieutenant asked me to bring them to you." She handed him the package, and he reached for his hat.

"Thank you." He opened the envelope and was relieved to see his mirrored sunglasses were intact, even though his phone had been smashed beyond use. He leafed through Caitlyn's pocketbook, and as far as he could tell, everything was in its place.

Colt set the items on the desk and stared at the detectives. "I can't imagine why someone in Scottsdale would want to hurt us, but we were borrowing the K9 vehicle from Officer Berkley, here. Dan, could you have been the target?"

Dan shrugged, but Webb answered, "Sure could have been. I suppose in some ways that's far more likely. Except that wouldn't explain why someone stole your dog. It's impossible to know if the two events are connected or not. We'll learn more when we find out who that truck belongs to."

5

Stella sat at her desk in the bay window of the bedroom she had shared with John for almost forty years. Faded wallpaper curled away from the painted trim, and she flicked it with her pen. She'd been trying to plan another trip for her and John to take. Their recent extended vacation to Ireland had breathed new life into their marriage, and she wanted to keep the magic going.

Only, as she gazed out at the mountains that surrounded their Wyoming home, she could only think of her daughter. No one, including Caitlyn, had known she was pregnant, though in retrospect Stella should have known. Caitlyn had been tired a lot, but Stella thought it was just because she had worked so hard to train for the K9 qualifications and the dog trials. Learning about the pregnancy and the loss was a double shock that pierced Stella deeply. That Renegade was missing only made everything worse.

She wanted to call Caitlyn, but debated on how much

of her own experience she should share. She hadn't talked about her own miscarriage in over thirty years. Yet even now, the dull edge of pain and emptiness scraped against her heart.

Stella tapped the end of her porcelain floral fountain pen on her pad of paper. Soreness spread through her chest as she remembered how debilitatingly sad she was those many years ago. She'd only carried the tiny life within her for eight weeks, but its loss caused an emotional chasm that had never fully healed.

John didn't understand. He was a practical cattle rancher, and like losing a calf, he saw the miscarriage as a sad but mixed blessing. He told her that there must have been something wrong with the fetus and that they'd get pregnant again as soon as the doctor thought it was safe. Stella sighed, releasing her remembered pain. She knew John had been trying to comfort her in his way, but he had missed the mark entirely, and she had felt alone in her grief for months.

She always wondered if the baby had been a boy or a girl. For years after the loss, she still teared up when a woman in a movie had a miscarriage And even now, Stella was reluctant to open the old wound, but she would do anything she could to give Caitlyn even a little comfort. She reached for her phone.

CAITLYN SLEPT FITFULLY during the late morning hours, not getting any proper rest because of her worry over Renegade and the heavy grief that suffocated her. The phone on her bedside table rang, and she lifted the receiver. "Hello?"

"Hi, honey. It's Mom. Can you talk?"

Caitlyn choked back a sob. Hearing her mother's voice dissolved all the strength she had been building up. Another whimper forced its way out of her throat.

"Oh, my darling girl. I'm so sorry. Don't hold back the tears. Is Colt there?"

"No," Caitlyn sniffed and reached for a tissue. "He went to the police department to help with the investigation."

"I wish I was there with you so I could give you the biggest hug. And I know you might not be ready to talk. Is it okay that I called?"

"Of course. I'm sorry about earlier."

"You have nothing to apologize for. I understand. On that note, I wanted to let you know something I've never told you." Stella drew in a deep breath. "I've been through what you're going through, too, and I'm here if you need me."

"You have?" Caitlyn grimaced at the smallness of her own voice. She couldn't stand sounding so weak. So needy.

"Yes, I have, and I hope you'll allow yourself some time to get through this. Losing a pregnancy, even in these early stages, is a devastating loss. You need to give yourself permission to grieve."

"But I didn't even know I was pregnant. I don't understand why it hurts so much."

"I know, sweetheart. But it does, and that's okay. Like

any other grief, it will be sharp some days and less so on others. It took me a long time to process everything."

"When did you miscarry, Mom?"

"Between Logan and you. It's one reason you brought me such joy when you were born."

"I'm sorry, Mom. I never knew." Caitlyn's breath skipped on a hiccup.

"Well, it's certainly not a club anyone wants to belong to, but it helps to talk through your feelings with other women who've had a similar experience."

"Thanks for telling me."

"I'm always here for you, and we'll talk more if you want to, when you get home. Have you had any news about Renegade?"

Caitlyn closed her eyes against another wave of pain. "No. Colt is helping with the search, but I have heard nothing back yet. I hate thinking of Ren out there somewhere, wondering where I am and why I'm not protecting him."

The door to her room opened, and Colt entered backward, pushing the door as he came in. When he turned, Caitlyn saw he carried two to-go bowls filled with chocolate ice cream and smothered with sauces and other goodies.

"Mom? Colt just walked in. He brought me an ice cream sundae, so I better go."

"Good for him. He's a good man. Go eat your treat and spend time with Colt. You two need each other. Call me later. I love you."

"Love you too, Mom. And thanks for sharing. It

means a lot." Caitlyn hung up and Colt handed her a bowl.

"I thought this might help cheer you up a little." He grinned.

She doubted even chocolate could ease her pain, but Colt was doing his best to care for her, and that meant everything. "Thanks. Any news on Ren?"

Colt's smile faltered. "Not yet. But there is evidence that the truck that hit us did so on purpose." Colt shared what he learned about the videotape of the blue Ford parked at the hotel before the accident.

"Do you think they were targeting us? That they followed us?"

"It's more likely they were stalking Officer Berkley. The Explorer we borrowed was assigned to him. He's who the driver of the truck would have expected to be driving it."

"I suppose that makes sense." Caitlyn took a huge bite of the cold, sticky-sweet dessert. The frozen goodness eased the constant ache in her throat.

Colt scooted her legs over so he could sit next to her on the bed. "Have you decided about the D&C?"

"Yes, I think so. On Blake's recommendation, I'm going to have it done. But then I want to get out of here."

"He also said you needed to rest."

"I have rested, and what I *need* is to find Ren. Every minute that goes by makes that less likely."

"Excuse me, for just a second." A nurse came into the room to check Caitlyn's stats. She noticed the sticky bowls. "Looks like someone sure loves you!" she said as she jotted down numbers on the whiteboard hanging on the wall. "Everything looks fine here. Doctor Whitman will be here in a few minutes."

The doctor arrived on the nurse's heels. "I spoke with Doctor Kennedy. He told me he discussed the procedure with you."

"Yes. After he looked at all your findings, we agreed that having the D&C is the right thing to do." Caitlyn fisted the bed sheet. "But I'd like to do it as soon as possible so I can get out of here."

Doctor Whitman touched Caitlyn's wrist and smiled compassionately. "I have a time slot open at three this afternoon, but you will need to spend the night in the hospital so we can monitor you. If all goes as expected, and you get some rest, I will most likely release you by late tomorrow morning. How does that sound?"

"Like I don't have much choice." Caitlyn sighed.

"Thank you," Colt stepped in. "Is it okay that Catie has ice cream in her stomach?"

"It isn't a problem, since we won't be giving her a general anesthetic. I think localized pain management will be enough. I'll send the nursing staff in to prep you around two o'clock."

"Thanks, Doc." Caitlyn scooped another dripping bite into her mouth. When the doctor left, she wiped her lips on a napkin and asked, "How are *you* doing, Colt? I know how much you wanted for us to have a baby. I'm sorry. I feel like I failed, somehow."

Colt's gold-flecked hazel eyes darkened with emotion, and he took her bowl from her, setting it on the bedside table. He gripped her wrists and pulled her toward him. Sliding his hands to her shoulders, he held her so he could look her straight in the eye. "You did not fail at anything. What happened was not your fault, in any way." He bent forward and kissed her forehead. He spoke against her skin. "I'm sad, and honestly surprised at how much it hurts." He drew back and searched her eyes. "But I'm more worried about you. I love you, Catie, and I'm so grateful that I didn't lose you, too." They clung to each other in a moment of shared grief.

Colt's pocket rang, and he shifted to pull out the phone. "Sorry to keep using this. Mine was destroyed in the accident, and I need to get a new one." He tapped the screen to answer. "Colt Branson, here."

"Sheriff Branson, this is Detective Webb. I'm calling to let you know we found the truck."

"That's good news. Where is it?"

"It's in a demolition yard. It showed up at one of the junk yards Berkley had alerted, and when it came in, the manager called us right away."

"What about the driver?"

"We don't have him yet. But we have his name and last known address. There's a unit on the way there now."

"I'm at the hospital with my wife, and I need to stay here while she undergoes a procedure. Keep me posted, will you?"

"You got it."

Colt sat in the chair by the bed and leaned forward. "They know who owned the truck that hit us."

"It was *light* blue, right?" Something tugged at the edge of Caitlyn's mind but refused to solidify. Why did that information seem poignant?

"Yeah. A 1996 Ford, F250."

6

———

Colt sat at a coffee shop in the hospital lobby, sipping a dark brew and letting the fragrant steam sooth him while he waited for the recovery nurse to inform him when Caitlyn's procedure was finished. The shop looked more like a cozy Starbucks than a hospital pit-stop. There were comfortable chairs gathered around a gas-fireplace, which seemed out of place in Arizona.

He scratched the itchy stubble covering his chin that reminded him he hadn't cleaned up since their accident the night before. Had it really been less than twenty-four hours since someone stole Renegade and started off this horrible series of events? First Ren, then an accident that both revealed and stole their baby in one fell swoop. Caitlyn having to go through a D&C on the heels of a serious concussion. It was sobering how fast their lives changed in such a short amount of time.

Caitlyn's phone rested on his table, and it buzzed with

a text from Allison, the mother of his ten-year-old son, Jace.

> Just reminding u, it's ur weekend with Jace. I'm txting you, because Colt never answered me, and I need to know what time ur picking up Jace?

Colt sighed. Allison obviously knew she could reach him through Caitlyn, and she also knew they were in Arizona. What he didn't understand was why Allison always had to be so prickly.

> This is Colt. We're stuck in AZ. My phone is dead. Doubt I'll be back by the wknd. Can we switch weeks?

> Figures… No, we can't. I have plans.

Fury rose behind Colt's eyes. He bit down on his lower lip and waited for the heat of his irritation to pass before he replied.

> I'm dealing with an emergency here. Catie and I were in a car accident last night. She's in the hospital and I don't have control over my time right now.

Three dots hovered over the text line, indicating Allison was typing. Finally,

> I heard about the baby, Colt. And I am sorry, but don't forget you already have a son, and he needs you.

Colt didn't think Allison could surprise him anymore with her insensitivity, but her comment was a gut punch. That the gossip chain had run through Moose Creek so fast was bad enough, but the fact that Allison knew about their loss and was still giving him crap was too much. He waited for the shock of her self-centeredness to subside so he wouldn't say words he'd regret before he typed,

> I'll figure something out and let you
> know.

He gulped a too-hot mouthful of coffee, and as it burned down his esophagus, he dialed Dylan. "Hey, are you and McKenzie going to be at the ranch this weekend?"

"I think so. Why? What do you need?"

"It's my weekend with Jace, and I don't know if we'll be home by then or not. I doubt it since Caitlyn won't be released until she's recovered from her procedure and the doctors are confident her concussion is on the mend. Plus, Caitlyn isn't leaving here until we find Renegade. Would you guys mind picking up Jace and keeping him at your place until we get there?" Colt hated to ask, especially on such short notice, but at least he knew Jace would love to hang out with his uncle.

"I'll check with Kenzie, but I don't think it will be a problem to have him. In fact, it sounds like fun. Mind if I take him riding or fishing?"

A distant but familiar female voice echoed in the background. "Tell Colt we'd be happy to have Jace over." A rustling noise came through the speaker, and

McKenzie spoke directly into the phone. "Hey Colt, how's Caitlyn feeling?"

Colt explained Caitlyn was having the D&C and that she'd probably get released the following day.

"How is her head?"

"Better, I think. Now if I can just get her to follow the concussion protocol."

"I'm so sorry, Colt. I wish I could say something to make things better."

"Thanks. I get it. I wish I had some magic words to help Caitlyn, too. You know how she is—she's trying to stuff the hurt and get back to work."

"I'm glad the doctor is keeping her overnight. On another note, I think Wes probably told you I have that gray pit bull you guys confiscated before you went to Arizona. He's at the kennel because Doctor Moore asked me to watch him for signs of aggression."

"Yeah? How's that going?"

"Good, actually. The poor dog has calmed down a lot since he got here. He's responding timidly to kindness with hope in his eyes, and I think he's beginning to trust me. He has displayed no dangerous behavior so far."

"Well, that's encouraging, but if he's not aggressive, why would he attack Jim's dog? That old Lab isn't a threat to anyone." Jim had been bringing his dog to the feed store with him every day since he was a puppy and in all those years, the dog had always behaved like the happy-go-lucky Labrador he is.

"Good question. Now that I'm able to get closer to Storm, I'm seeing signs of abuse. His neck is raw in places and scabbing over from wounds caused by the brutal collar he had on. His ears have some tearing, and there are scars on his body that appear to be bite marks.

"Storm?"

McKenzie chuckled. "It's just the name I've given him while he's here. I can't just call him 'Hey, you,' can I?"

Colt smiled, thinking of how much McKenzie loved dogs. "Do you think he—Storm—attacks other animals regularly?"

"Perhaps, but since he isn't showing aggression toward any of my dogs here, it makes me wonder if his owner was training him to be mean—maybe pitting him against other dogs to prove how tough he is. In either case, he might go after another dog, but probably only if he thought he had no other choice."

"I can't imagine Jim's old Lab trying to attack anyone. So, what explains the pit bull's aggression toward him?"

"Honestly, I think it has far more to do with his owner —that burly guy who Wes arrested. He was the threat, not the Lab."

"So, in your professional opinion, do you believe it's possible to re-home the pit?"

"I think there's a good possibility, but I'll keep him here and work with him until I'm sure."

"Thanks for the information. I'll check in with Wes and see what he's learned. And thank you for watching Jace for me, too. I'm sorry for the short notice, but hopefully we'll be home before too long."

"Just find Renegade. Caitlyn won't feel better until you do."

Colt dialed the phone that he and Allison agreed Jace could have for emergencies. It was an old flip phone with no video capabilities, and they had installed an app that only allowed five numbers to call or be called: His, Allison's, Caitlyn's, Allison's mother's, and Stella's.

"Hi Caitlyn!" Jace's exuberant energy bounced through the line.

"Hey, buddy. It's not Caitlyn. It's Dad on Caitlyn's phone. I wanted to let you know, we're okay, but Caitlyn and I were in a car accident. We're fine, but I won't be home in time to pick you up for the weekend."

"Oh. Okay." Disappointment chased away his son's cheerful tone. "I'm glad you're okay."

"Thanks, bud. I'm sorry I can't be there, but I asked Uncle Dylan to come get you and take you to the ranch until we can get there. Is that okay?"

The joy returned. "Yeah! Cool!"

Colt grinned. "Good. Same pickup time, same pickup place, and Caitlyn and I will be home as soon as we can." He didn't bring up the fact that Renegade was missing. There was no reason to upset Jace before they had any answers.

7

———

McKenzie handed Dylan's phone back and wandered toward the outdoor kennels. Tall grasses grew up along the fences that would need trimming before winter set in. The assorted dogs in her care either wagged their tails or jumped up to greet her as she walked down the row. It was time for her least favorite job—cleaning the pens. She spoke with the furry crew as she gathered her shovel, rake, and trash can.

Her original plan was to run a Belgian Malinois breeding facility and train the puppies as police dogs, but somehow, alongside that, she had collected an assorted menagerie of rescue dogs from all over Wyoming.

The local vet called her anytime there was a need for canine housing, and the new gray pit bull whom she had named Storm, along with his partner in crime, Chance, a liver-and-white-spotted pit bull were two of his recent rescues. She kept them on the other end of the row of kennels. They were her first rehab animals, and they didn't seem to get along. When they were in proximity of one another, they growled and snapped at each other. Two things were certain; they both needed a lot of love and attention, and they were slowly beginning to trust her.

Storm reportedly was the dog who had attacked Jim's old dog down at the feed store. The Lab had a few scratches after the incident, but overall, he was fine. Storm had injuries too, but his had been there long enough to heal. He was fine except for a tender ring rubbed raw around his neck by the pronged collar he'd been wearing when Colt and his deputy, Wes, found the two dogs chained up in a yard on the outskirts of town.

McKenzie had witnessed no signs of aggression from Storm so far, but who knew what kind of mental and emotional wounds the poor dog bore or when they might show up? But the chunks missing from his ears and the scars on his muzzle and neck told a sickening story.

Storm got to his feet as she walked down the aisle toward his pen. His tail wagged tentatively, but he peered up at her with sad eyes. "Hiya, Storm." McKenzie squatted in front of his gate. "You poor guy. I sure wish you could tell me all you've been through, and that you understood how much I want to help you."

"He does," her father-in-law, John's, voice floated over her head, and she jumped. "You can tell by the way he's happy to see you."

Shooting to her feet, McKenzie pressed a hand to her racing heart. "John. I didn't see you there."

"Sorry I startled you. I'm waiting out here for Dylan to

decide to get back to work. Thought I'd check on the dogs while I was at it."

"Dylan's already been out this morning. He came in for a quick break, and Colt called, so it took him a little longer than usual."

"Stella talked with Caitlyn a while ago, too. Sad business."

"It is." McKenzie couldn't begin to imagine what Caitlyn was feeling. "Are you going out on the range with Dylan this afternoon?"

Dylan stepped out of the kennel office and walked toward them, gravel crunching under his boots. "Hey Dad, what are you doing down here?"

"Waiting for you."

"Well, I don't have time to chat. I've got Sampson saddled and ready to head back out. Riding the fences today. Did you need something?"

"Thought I'd ride out with you, is all." John adjusted his hat.

Dylan exhaled a long breath, and the muscles of his jaw bunched. "You're not gonna gripe all day about the way I'm doing things around here, are you? Because I'm doing just fine."

"Only a fool stops learning, son." John headed toward the barn, presumably to tack up his horse.

Dylan raised a brow as his gaze followed his dad's steps. "There goes my peaceful afternoon."

McKenzie slid her hand into the crook of Dylan's elbow. "Maybe it would have gone better if you hadn't come across quite so defensively."

"Look, Kenze, I don't need crap from you, too."

"Hey—I'm not trying to give you a hard time. I know he's been difficult to deal with lately." She hated that John offered no credit to Dylan for all the hard work he did to keep the family ranch running. It seemed like her father-in-law only saw Dylan's flaws.

"Yeah, well. I'd rather I was on my own today. Dad has been complaining about the way I do things around here ever since they got home from Ireland. He seems to forget that he's the one who taught me all I know."

McKenzie chuckled. "I think he's bored and feels useless. Maybe you could set him up with a project—something that keeps him busy and out of your hair."

"That's not a bad idea." Dylan bent to kiss McKenzie on the top of her head. "By the way, there was a message on the office phone from Doctor Moore."

"Oh? What did he want?"

"He was checking on the pit bulls, and he also said he had Athena's test results back."

McKenzie bounced on her toes. "And? What are they? Did he say?"

A sly grin pressed across Dylan's mouth. "Looks like you're going to be a doggy-grandma!"

"Really?" McKenzie clapped her hands together before throwing her arms around Dylan's neck. He smelled of the fresh Wyoming air that surrounded them. "That's so exciting! I wasn't sure since Renegade only spent a few days with her. This is the best news ever!" Yet, the thought of telling Caitlyn made McKenzie feel like someone dumped an ice bucket on her head. "Except with Caitlyn and Colt's heartbreaking loss, along with the fact that Ren is missing, do you think I should tell them Athena is expecting Ren's puppies?"

"I'd wait until this all settles out. With any luck, they will find Renegade, safe and sound, and then they'll all come home. Then, the pending litter will be welcome news." Her husband's expression did not convey the hope of his words.

"What if they don't find him, Dyl? It will destroy Caitlyn, especially now..."

"I don't even want to think about that, but if that happens, maybe you could train up one of his puppies for her. That might give her some small solace."

As close as Renegade and Caitlyn were, she doubted it. McKenzie pulled a long piece of grass from its sheath and chewed on the tender end while she thought about her sister-in-law, her best friend. She noticed Stella on her way to the barn. When she got there, Stella stood in the breezeway, silhouetted against the light coming through from the other side of the building. John's shadowed figure joined her, and he gathered his wife in his arms, took off his hat, and kissed her passionately.

Dylan pulled his phone from the holder on his belt. "I'm going to call Caitlyn to see how she's doing before I ride out."

"Dylan!" McKenzie whispered harshly as she tugged on his sleeve.

"What?" his voice boomed in return.

She rolled her eyes and held her index finger to her lips. "Shh! Look!" She pointed to the barn.

Dylan's mouth opened before his eyebrows rose. His expression softened, and a half grin appeared under his dark mustache. "Well, that's not something I've seen in a long time. Looks like their vacation brought back some magic."

"I think it's wonderful. I hope you and I are still kissing like that when we're grandparents," McKenzie said on a sigh.

Dylan scooped her into his arms and nuzzled her neck, tickling her with his beard. "We need to keep working on becoming parents first."

She giggled and slid her fingers into his hair. "Well, let's have an early dinner tonight and see what happens later."

8

Other than some cramping, and the pressure from a persistent headache she'd had since the procedure, Caitlyn felt well enough to go out and search for Ren. As soon as the nurse left the room, Caitlyn opened the drawer of the side table where they stored her personal items. She pulled her jeans from the plastic hospital bag and thrust one foot into the leg.

The room door swung open, and Colt peered around it. "Hey, what are you doing? You need to get back in bed."

Dizzy, Caitlyn swayed, and Colt hurried to steady her. She tugged free from his grasp. "I feel fine, and we're wasting time."

Colt gripped her shoulder firmly. "Catie, the local cops are on top of finding the guy who smashed into us." She didn't persuade him with her tough-guy attitude, and taking her elbow, he guided her back to the bed.

"I don't care who ran into us. I want to find Renegade." Reluctantly, Caitlyn allowed Colt to pull the blanket over her legs.

"All the Scottsdale cops are looking for him, Catie. You need to stay in bed until the doctor says otherwise. You won't be any use to Ren if you pass out in the middle of the street."

"That's unlikely." She pressed her throbbing head against her pillow. "I have something I wanted to tell you, though. The truck that hit us—the one in the video? I think I recognize it."

Suddenly alert, Colt asked, "What do you mean?"

"Remember the day we first got to the dog trials, and that jerk ran into me in the parking lot?"

"Yeah. I recall that guy because you wouldn't let me kick his ass."

"Well, I probably should have let you. Wasn't he driving a light blue, older model Ford?"

Colt scrunched his brows in thought. "I don't remember."

Caitlyn's phone vibrated, and Colt reached for it, looked at the call and handed it to her. "It's Dylan."

She took a deep, steadying breath, not wanting to deal with any pussyfooting from her big brother, no matter how kind he was going to be. "Hey, Dyl. What's up?"

"You're what's up. How are you feeling?"

"I'm fine, but they won't let me leave the hospital to find Renegade, so I'm mostly pissed off."

"Don't be a pain in the doctor's ass. They're trying to take care of you is all, and you need to let them."

Caitlyn relaxed at her brother's rebuff. At least he wasn't dripping with sympathy that she didn't want. "Yeah, yeah. Colt just made me get back in bed. But tomorrow, I'll be out looking for my dog."

"Well, you sound as feisty as usual. They'll be begging you to leave by morning." He paused. "Listen, kiddo. I'm sorry about what happened."

Her throat clogged with a rush of emotion. "I know."

"Okay. Call me tomorrow to keep us posted."

"We will." Caitlyn bit down on her lip. "Thanks, Dyl." She was relieved by his abruptness. He knew she hated emotional conversations. It was good enough that he called to check on her.

"Love you."

"Yep. Me too." She tapped "end" and tossed her phone onto the bed. To give her hands something to do, she reached for the plastic hairbrush that came inside the complimentary toiletry kit and tore it through the tangles of her long hair.

"Whoa." Colt grasped her hand and unwrapped her fisted fingers from the brush handle. "Here, let me." He lifted the mass of her hair, and, as soft as if he were petting a kitten, he brushed the snarls from her tresses. The sweetness of the act made her cry.

Colt set the brush down and held her while sorrow flowed from her heart. He kept her tucked safe and warm against his chest until there were no more tears.

COLT WAS both furious and frustrated with his complete inability to help Caitlyn. He should be able to do something to make her feel better, but he was barely grappling with his own emotions. He vacillated between deep grief and red-hot anger. Right now, he was seething at the man who crashed into them and killed their baby. He would find the asshole and make him pay.

Caitlyn's phone buzzed again, and she reached for it. "It's Logan." Her exhausted, tear-stained eyes looked up at him. "I don't know if I can do this."

"Do you want me to talk to him?"

"Would you mind?"

He took her cell and answered. "Hey, Logan. It's Colt."

"Hey, man. Can't tell you how sorry I am about the baby."

Colt swallowed and was thankful Caitlyn didn't have to face Logan's directness. "Thanks. It was a shock."

"I bet. How's my little sister doing?"

"Doing her best to tough it out. Did you hear about Renegade?"

"Yeah, I just got off the phone with my mom. Any news?"

Colt stroked the length of Caitlyn's dark brown hair. "No, not yet. We got a lead on the guy who hit us last night, and we're trying to determine if there was a connection between him and the K9 cop whose car we were borrowing."

"Is there any way I can help your investigation?" Logan was an FBI K9 agent in Denver, and sometimes he used the databases he had access to for assisting Colt's law enforcement work in Wyoming.

"Not right now, but if anything comes up, I'll call you."

"Good. Listen, I originally called my mom to tell her that Addison and I want to get married at Christmastime on the ranch."

"Congratulations. That's great news. I know that will give Catie something to be glad about."

"Yeah, but for now, tell her I'm here if she needs me and please remind her that her dog is smart and resilient. You'll find him."

"Thanks, Logan."

Colt paraphrased the conversation to Caitlyn.

A ghost of a smile brushed across her lips. "That is happy news. I bet my mom is thrilled. You know how she loves to plan big events."

"Absolutely. A wedding will keep her occupied, but it's too bad it won't give your dad something to do."

"Why do you say that?"

Colt shrugged. "I hear he's been micro-managing Dylan—giving him a hard time about the decisions he makes for the ranch."

Caitlyn nodded and hugged her knees up to her chin. "Sounds about right. I know when mom and dad were traveling it was a pleasant break for Dylan." She stretched with a massive yawn.

Colt swept her soft cheek with his work-worn thumb. "You need to get some rest."

A peach-filtered light had filled the room, and Colt glanced out the window. The beauty of the sunset took him by surprise. "Catie, look at this."

She turned but didn't have the full view, so Colt lifted her and carried her to a seat by the glass. He eased onto the chair and rested her on his lap. A deep tangerine orb wavered on the bare brown-mountain horizon, sending shards of gold and orange through fluffy white clouds that floated in the cerulean sky.

"Glorious," Colt murmured as he watched the shafts of sunlight piercing the misty pillows.

Minutes later, Caitlyn replied, "Hope."

9

———

Stella glimpsed John's suggestive smile in the lamplight as she slid her nightgown over her head. After all these years, her husband still found her attractive, and it warmed her heart and sent a kaleidoscope of butterflies to flight in her stomach.

She pressed her belly and said, "I had an interesting visit with McKenzie while you and Dylan were out on the ranch today."

"Oh, yeah?" John sat in his chair with his legs stretched out long. He sipped his favorite single-malt as he lazily watched her dress for bed.

"She told me you and Dylan have been at each other's throats lately."

"That's a little strong."

"Not according to McKenzie. What's the problem between you two?"

"I just don't believe Dylan thinks all the way through the decisions he makes. He takes too many risks, hoping to make a profit. I don't want him losing all we've worked for over the years."

"Is there something he's not getting done? He works so hard, and I thought he'd turned things around and was doing a great job managing the ranch. You said so yourself when we were in Ireland."

Their Ireland trip was something she'd really had to fight for. Convincing her husband to leave his beloved ranch was like pulling burrs from a horse's mane. He was so stubborn that in the end she had threatened to go on the trip alone.

At the time, she and John were struggling in their relationship. With all the changes that came from him retiring from ranch work to Dylan taking over, their marriage took the brunt of the stress and had almost become a casualty. She thought their flame had extinguished. But in the end, she persuaded John to travel with her, and they rekindled their love and passion along the journey.

"I suppose I did." He stood and approached her, running his fingers through her hair before he rested his rough hands on her shoulders.

Stella met his amber eyes, seeing desire swirling in them. She looped her arms around his waist. "I think maybe you need a new focus. Let Dylan do the job you trained him his whole life to do and find something different to occupy yourself with."

"Like what?" He kissed her neck.

Smiling, she said, "I know you love fishing and hunting. What about golf? You could learn how to play up at the country club."

"I do like fishing..."

"Dylan and McKenzie are watching Jace for Colt this weekend. Why don't you take our grandson up to the river? Do grandpa things."

A smile lit his granite features. "Now there's a fine idea."

"Actually, I was thinking maybe we all could go. You and Dylan both need a break from work, and I thought we could have a campfire cookout. I bet Jace would love it."

"I would too."

Stella turned and reached for her brush on the dressing table. John took it from her and ran it through her graying hair. When had she lost so much color? She hardly recognized her own lined face in the mirror anymore. She spoke to John in the reflection. "I talked to Logan this afternoon, too."

"What's that young buck up to?"

"He and Addison have finally set a date."

"It's about time they made it official. When?"

"Christmas." Stella loved the idea of a romantic snowy wedding.

She pictured Addison's short dark curls filling with fat snowflakes as they bounced above a white fur-lined cape. And Logan, handsome in a black tux, gazing at his bride. Stella chuckled at herself. She'd become such a softy at her age. Stella was disappointed that she and John would have to postpone their trip, especially since he was excited as she was to travel this time, but she didn't want anything to get in the way of their middle son's wedding.

"Did you tell them we'd be out of town?"

"No. I figured we could change our travel dates. Maybe push the trip out until the new year. You don't mind, do you?"

John set the brush down and picked up his glass. He knocked back a large swallow and crossed the room to the decanter for a refill. "I was looking forward to bringing in the new year with you in Malta."

"I know. Me too. But I don't want to spoil the kids' plans. A Christmas wedding on the ranch will be beautiful."

"They're planning on getting hitched up here?" John returned to the back of her chair and, setting his tumbler on her vanity table, he met her gaze in the mirror. "That'll be nice." He murmured as he unclasped her necklace, piling the chain next to his glass. Her heart picked up its pace.

"Yes. And we can still go to Malta—maybe for Valentine's day." She couldn't help smiling in response to the simmering heat that hovered in his eyes.

John bent to kiss her temple as he massaged her shoulders, and she placed her hands on top of his, enjoying their strength. He slid his fingers along the lacy neckline of her gown to her throat and tilted her head up so he could kiss her lips.

"Come to bed," the scotch drenched words echoed inside her mouth, sending an electric pulse to her core. She took the hand he offered and followed him into the night.

10

───────

McKenzie always did her best thinking when she was cleaning out the dog kennels. Dylan told her that mucking stalls was the same for him. She supposed it was the mindless productivity that leant itself to ruminating. That morning, the mountain air was crisp and invigorating, but her thoughts wrestled with the tension vibrating between her husband and his father. It hurt her that John refused to acknowledge the bone-wearying work that Dylan put in on the ranch. Their cattle business was more profitable than it had been in years, and it was Dylan who had brought the ranch back from the brink of bankruptcy.

She leaned on the long handle of her pooper-scooper and watched Dylan as he fed the dogs for her. He was a seamless part of this place and the rugged mountains that surrounded them. She smiled, appreciating his fresh haircut and beard trim he got the day before. He tended to get a little scruffy after a while, but wow—he sure cleaned up nice. Her gaze caressed his firm jaw and the muscles bunching under his shirt as he worked. Her body warmed as she watched him. As if he had read her mind, he glanced at her and winked.

"When do you need to pick up Jace?" she asked, trying to cover for her lusty thoughts.

"'Round lunchtime. Thought I'd take him to the café for a burger. Want to come?"

"Sure. I think I'll be done by then."

He bobbed his head. "I've been thinking about training up a horse for Jace."

"Wow. That's quite a gift."

"It's practical for him to have a horse he can ride when he's here. Things are different on a ranch. It's not like I'm giving him a pony to spoil him. He's getting too big to be riding double when Colt's out here. It's time he gets better at riding on his own so we can all go out together."

"Shouldn't you talk to Colt about it first?"

Dylan gave her a bemused look. "I don't know why. Colt will agree."

"You sound awfully certain, but he might have to speak with Allison about it."

He shrugged her comment away, and McKenzie knew to expect another horse on the property in the near future. "By the way, your mom called this morning."

"Oh, yeah? What was so urgent she couldn't just walk over?"

"Nothing. She asked if we'd like to go on a fishing trip with her, your dad, and Jace tomorrow. She's making plans for a campfire cookout."

"Sounds good. Nobody can cook over a fire like my

mama. She can even bake a cake over the coals. It sounds like a plan, but it'll mean working late today, though."

"Anything I can do to help?"

"Maybe you could go get Jace. I'll need to work through lunch."

"Dylan, it's okay to take a break."

"Sure, if I don't mind listening to my dad harp on me about not getting the work done."

McKenzie let out a sigh and went back to scooping dog messes and raking the kennels. Dylan finished filling all the bowls with kibble and turned toward the barn. Before he left, she braved a topic that often hung between them. "You know, I feel awful for what your sister is going through with the miscarriage and all…"

Dylan stopped to look at her over his shoulder. "And?"

"It just feels weird. I mean, it doesn't seem fair. She wasn't even *aware that* she was pregnant, and we've been trying for over a year." She kept her gaze on the rake.

"Well, it sure as hell isn't fair that she lost her baby." His voice was low and edged in warning. "I'm not sure what you're trying to say."

She wasn't exactly sure what she was trying to say either, and she definitely didn't want to get into an argument with Dylan. "No, of course, what happened is tragic. But—I don't know—I guess, if she'd been paying more attention… Look, I'm saying this all wrong. What I mean is, I wish we could get pregnant. But what if there's something wrong with me?"

"There is nothing wrong with you." Dylan spun on his heel and approached her. He touched her chin and tilted her face to his. "You said the home pregnancy test you took was positive, right?"

"Yes, but you know we've had a positive result before, only to find out they were wrong."

"Sometimes it takes a while, honey. But if you're worried, why don't you make an appointment to see Doc Kennedy?"

"Blake?" Her face heated at the thought. "I'm thinking of seeing a doctor in Spearfish. I'd rather see someone there."

"What's wrong with Blake? He's a good doctor, and he's right here in town."

"Nothing's wrong with him except he's our friend and *way* too good looking to be taken seriously as an OB/GYN." She would die before she lay on an exam table in a paper gown with her heels in metal stirrups in front of Blake Kennedy. McKenzie pulled her collar open to get some cool air on her neck.

Dylan chuckled. "I don't have anything to worry about, do I? Do you have a crush on the town doctor? Maybe I should insist that you see a woman doctor."

"Honestly? I would be much more comfortable with that. But what about you? You could see Blake."

"Why would *I* want to see Blake?"

"Shouldn't you see a doctor, too?"

His eyes narrowed. "What for? My plumbing is working fine. Besides, I think you're worrying over nothing. Let's see what your doctor says."

11

———————

Colt had a rental car delivered to the hospital and went to collect their things from their original hotel. He packed Renegade's collapsible kennel in the trunk along with their suitcases and the rest of the dog gear. He carried into their new hotel room only what Caitlyn might need over the next few hours.

She shrugged him off when he offered to help her walk inside, but she held his hand and looked him in the eye. "Colt, I don't want to stay here while you go to the demolition yard. I have to be part of the search."

"You will, Catie, but we won't find Ren at the junkyard. You must rest so that you'll be ready to look for him when we have more information."

"Colt—"

He held up a hand to cut her off. "I mean it, Catie. I understand how you're feeling, but I'm not taking you with me this morning. If you rest while I meet with Detectives Webb and Albrecht at the demolition lot, then we can go out to search for Renegade when I get back. Okay?"

Colt had learned that attempting to put his foot down with Caitlyn often ended up with her stubbornly doing whatever it was he didn't want. But he wasn't budging this time.

"I'll be back by lunchtime. Okay?"

Caitlyn glared at him, but he stood his ground. She could be as stubborn as an ox when she wanted something, and he usually stayed out of her way, but not today. He knew Caitlyn's heart was broken, and that she was scared for Renegade. She was under a tremendous amount of stress, both physically and emotionally, but she wouldn't bother to take care of herself if he didn't insist.

"Why don't you get into bed? You can't watch TV, but can I get you anything else?"

"No," she answered, and threw back the covers and climbed onto the mattress, yanking the blankets to cover her legs. Crossing her arms over her chest, she let out an angry huff. "Happy?"

"Yes. Now stay put until I return." Colt sat next to her on the edge of the mattress. "I won't be long. Please rest. We're going to need your expertise when we find the guy who crashed that truck into us. And Renegade needs you energized and alert."

"I hear you, and I'll try to sleep, but you better get back here soon. And keep me posted."

He brushed her cheek with his fingers, and holding her jaw, he kissed her softly. "I love you, Catie."

Some of the tension in her shoulders relaxed. "I love you, too."

Before Colt left, he got her a bottle of water from the mini-bar and promised to be back as fast as he could. He drove the rental Camry out to the wrecking yard out on highway 202, where local cops located the Ford Truck.

He parked behind the detectives' unmarked sedan. The men stood next to the smashed-up vehicle wearing short-sleeved shirts and ties. Even though it was late October, the Arizona heat was too intense for suit coats. The truck's crushed hood buckled up into the cab, and all that remained of the windshield was a web of cracked safety glass hanging from the frame. An image of the second before impact flashed across Colt's mind careening together with the memory of the sound of twisting metal and he shivered.

"So, this is it, huh?" Colt spoke over the sound of squealing metal to address both men, happy that he could hide his emotion behind his mirrored lenses. "It's amazing the driver survived, let alone drove away."

"We're pretty sure this is the Ford that hit you." Webb stretched his long arms and then scratched his chin. "The paint matches the Explorer, and the damage lines up, too. Of course, we'll have to wait for verification from the lab to be certain. For now, we need to contact the owner and interview him. You never know. Maybe someone stole his truck."

Albrecht perched his hands on his hips. "That's probably what he'll try to tell us, anyway." He shaded his eyes and peered up at Colt. "How's the wife?"

Colt chuffed, thinking how much Caitlyn would hate

being referred to as *the wife*. "She's out of the hospital and is at the new hotel room, resting."

"Good. Glad she's going to be okay. Looking at that truck, I'd say you're both lucky to be alive."

"Yeah. Now, let's bring this dirtbag in. I want to know why he was after us, or if it was Berkley he was after the whole time."

Webb held up an Arizona license plate. "We got all we need. There was nothing left in the cab or glovebox, and we've had it dusted for prints. But we can find him with this."

"I already called it in." Albrecht rolled forward on his toes, making himself an inch taller for a second. "We should have a name and address any minute."

"And any criminal history, too." Colt clapped a hand on the back of his sweaty neck. It was beyond his understanding how people could live in such a hot, dry climate year-round. He couldn't wait to get inside the air-conditioned car. Wiping a trickle of sweat from his temple, he said, "I want to hear from him why he smashed into the Explorer—who he was targeting, and why."

Webb's dark eyes assessed Colt. "It's been an unusually hot fall here, and you look like you're going to melt right into the dirt. Why don't you go sit in the AC?" The tall detective's phone buzzed with a text he read silently. "Got him. The truck belongs to a man named Melville Rankin—lives down in South Mountain. I'll text you the address."

Colt entered the information into Google Maps. "Looks like I'll be driving right past our hotel on the way.

I'm going to stop in and check on my wife. Then, I'll meet you there."

Caitlyn tried to nap, but sleep eluded her. What she needed was a steaming shower, and then if Colt wasn't back, she planned to go out and search for Ren on her own. She turned the water on and undressed while she waited for it to get hot. Staring at herself in the mirror, she ran her fingers over the dark bruises on the side of her face and body. She rested her hand on her flat abdomen, and guilt pressed its suffocating weight against her chest. She had been carrying a precious life and didn't even know it. Didn't have any moments of connection or wonder. Shouldn't she have known—have sensed a change? If she had, she would have been more careful. Eaten better... something.

Turning away from her own accusatory glare, she punished herself with the now too-hot water. Her skin reddened, and her emotions swelled to the surface. Her throat ached, and she leaned her forehead against the cool tile wall. Tears flooded her eyes, blending with the shower spray, and she let go of great sobs she couldn't hold in any longer.

Caitlyn didn't know how long she'd been standing under the water when she heard Colt call her name, but the water had gone cold. The bathroom door opened, and their eyes met through the glass shower door.

Colt's brows dipped, and his lips parted for a second before he clamped his jaws closed and swallowed. He opened the door and stepped in, pulling her into his arms. She fell into him, and he held her tight to his chest, not bothering with the fact that his clothes were getting soaked. He stroked her head and murmured comforting sounds she couldn't make out.

"I'm so sorry, Colt."

He drew back and tilted her chin so he could look her in the eyes; his sandy lashes spiked with water droplets. "I understand you being sad. I'm sad too. But you have nothing whatsoever to be sorry about. None of this was your fault, or mine. It was an accident we couldn't have prevented." He helped her out of the shower and wrapped her in a fluffy white towel. Taking another, he blotted her face.

"We found the name and address of the guy who owns the truck that hit us. I was on my way to meet the detectives there but stopped in to check on you. I'm glad I did." Colt kissed her forehead and kept his lips pressed against her damp skin.

"I'm coming with you." Caitlyn straightened her spine and pushed her shoulders back. "I can be ready in five. Besides, you need to change now, too."

Grinning up at her, Colt looked at his clothes as though he just realized he was drenched. "Guess that'd be a good idea."

She threw her arms around him. "I love you so much. Thank you for taking such great care of me." She tightened her towel and wrapped her hair in another before she gathered her jeans and T-shirt. "Let's go find this guy. He may have information about where Renegade is."

12

───────

Blake sat behind his desk in the clinic but was not inclined to work. Completely sated, he would have stayed in bed all day with the wildcat he left there, if he could. Heat flared up his neck when he thought of how they had wrecked his sheets last night. They never did go back to the cheesecake for their other dessert. At least not until morning, when they shared a slice of the creamy, strawberry covered cake with coffee. He wiped the Cheshire Cat grin from his face and gathered the files to go on his rounds.

One of the best parts of the evening was that he hadn't thought of Caitlyn at all. Though, now in the light of day, he was worried about her again. As soon as he finished seeing his patients, he'd call Doctor Whitman to discuss how the procedure went. Then, he'd call Caitlyn. But only to ask how she was feeling. He'd keep it strictly professional.

Like an addict, the minute he returned to his office, he called his house in search of a fix.

A sleepy feminine voice answered his phone. "Hello?"

"Hey, beautiful."

"Miss me already?"

"You know it. Last night was magic. I can't think about anything else."

"I like the sound of that," she purred.

"Can I see you again tonight? We could have dinner and maybe go to your place after?"

"I'm busy tonight."

"Oh, okay." A jab of discouragement surprised him. How quickly he'd become reliant on not feeling lonely.

"Let me check on something. I might be able to arrange a few things. Can you call me later?"

Relief surged through him in a wave of hope. "Sure. I'll call around lunchtime." He paused at his desk considering his emotional response, not sure if it was the specific woman he wanted to see or if he simply didn't want to face another evening alone.

After a call with Doctor Whitman, Blake reviewed Caitlyn's records. Everything looked in order. No reason for concern, yet he had to hear her voice. He needed reassurance from her she was okay. He knew Caitlyn would tell him what she thought he would like to hear, but he knew her well enough to sense if there were any issues under the surface.

He dialed Caitlyn's number but after three rings, his call went to voicemail. Disappointment weighed down on him as he hung up and texted her instead.

> Good morning. I just read through your files from Dr. Whitman. Looks as though the procedure went well. Everything seems in order. Call me when you get a minute. I'd like to hear from you how you're feeling.

Later, on his lunch break, Blake called the new woman in his life. "How's it looking for tonight?"

"I managed to free up my schedule. What did you have in mind?"

"I thought I could come to your place. Maybe we could order in. Do you like Chinese?"

"That won't work. We can't go to my house."

"Why not? Are you afraid to be seen with me?" he teased, but at the same time realized he still wasn't ready to make their relationship public.

"No, of course not, silly. But I have a roommate and we wouldn't have any privacy. And besides, you were the one who wanted to keep our friendship under wraps."

And under the covers. He grinned to himself. "We could always go to my house again then, or... I have an idea. Why don't we drive over to Sheridan for the night?"

"For the night?" Her voice took on a sultry lilt. "What's the matter, handsome? Didn't get enough last night?"

"I don't think that's possible."

She giggled. "I have some errands to do in Gillette today. How about we meet there at Hancock's Bar and Grille? You can pretend like you're picking me up at the bar."

"I can't wait. See you tonight."

Blake called his admin into his office and asked her to reschedule all his appointments for the following day. After work, he checked the weather for the next few days. No snow in the forecast meant he could take his Porsche on their getaway.

He zipped home to pack an over-night bag and let his answering service know he'd be out of town for a couple of days. The only call he wanted them to let through was the one he expected from Caitlyn. On his way out the door, he grabbed a bottle of champagne and two glasses. He wrapped them in a towel and stuffed them into his bag.

He parked at the back of the lot, away from the dirty trucks and other cars which were closer but might ding the shiny black paint on his car. As he walked toward the restaurant, he saw the blonde curls of his date bouncing as she laughed at something a man sitting next to her said. A smile warmed his lips. She was certainly an attractive diversion. It didn't surprise him to see other men trying to pick up on her. In fact, it made him feel proud.

Blake entered the bar with a confidence born of his status and looks. He noticed the feminine eyes that turned toward him and the behind-the-hand comments made to their girlfriends. He didn't think he was arrogant about the fortune of his bone structure, but he'd be lying if he said he didn't know that women thought he was handsome. His appearance was a card he'd learned at an early age to play when it suited him.

He approached her from behind, sliding his fingers into her soft curls. Leaning between her and the man who was hoping for a chance with her, Blake kissed her thoroughly.

She leaned back, a little breathless, and lazily blinked her eyes at him. "Well, hello to you, too."

Blake glanced at the man who had been chatting her up. "Thanks for keeping my place warm."

"Sorry, man. I didn't know she was with anyone."

"Not a problem."

The would-be suitor peeled away to look for another opportunity, and Blake took his seat. "I thought about you all day today. Are you ready for dinner? Or would you like another drink?"

She ran her hand down his sleeve. "I was thinking we should just stay in Gillette tonight. No need to drive all the way over to Sheridan. Besides, I was hoping we could have a little appetizer before dinner." She winked at him, leaving no doubt what she had in mind for a pre-meal starter.

"I like how you think." Blake slid his phone out and made a new hotel reservation. He grinned, "Ready whenever you are."

"Are we staying at a place with room service?"

"Of course."

"Good. Then let's have a night in."

Blake reached for her coat and helped her into it, appreciating the puff of perfume that filled the air when the coat settled onto her shoulders. He escorted her to the door, doing his best to keep his pace casual.

. . .

AFTER A DECADENT NIGHT rich in champagne, food, and sex, Blake slept like the dead. There had been no dreams filled with the dark-haired, dark-eyed beauty who often haunted his sleep. It occurred to him as he woke to a hot-pink fingernail swirling circles in his chest hair, that Caitlyn had never returned his call.

"Good morning, sleepyhead," she cooed.

"Morning, gorgeous." She reminded him of a 1950s blonde bombshell with her tousled bedhead. He reached for her, and kissing her, he pulled her on top of him.

An hour later, Blake showered and threw on one of the complimentary robes that hung in the closet.

"Hey," he trailed his fingers over a bare shoulder peeking out from under the covers. "I realize it's probably way too soon to ask you something like this, and you may feel like I'm being too forward, but what are you doing for Christmas?"

"Christmas? It isn't even Thanksgiving yet," she giggled.

"I'm spending Christmas week at a chalet in Vail. Come with me."

13

Caitlyn and Colt pulled up behind Detective Webb's sedan in the rundown neighborhood in South Mountain. The houses were one of four repeated designs, all single story with large front windows and no garages. The detectives stood in the bare yard of the house where Melville Rankin reportedly lived. Albrecht nodded, acknowledging their arrival while Webb spoke on his phone.

Caitlyn got out of the car. She adjusted the strap on her shoulder holster until her gun nestled comfortably against her body and waited for Colt to come around the hood before they approached the cops. "Isn't he here?"

"No," Albrecht stepped forward and held his hand out to her. "I'm J.D. Albrecht. Sorry about your accident."

Caitlyn bobbed her chin and kept her gaze steady— glad she could hide any errant emotions behind the reflective lenses of her aviator sunglasses. "Any idea where he is? Is he at work?" Her phone rang, and she glanced at the screen. It was Blake. Caitlyn sent his call to voicemail. She couldn't deal with him right then.

"Not only is Rankin not here, but it looks like he's moved. Webb is talking to the landlord now."

"Can you show me the photo on Rankin's driver's license?" A text from Blake buzzed through. Caitlyn read it and shook her head. She'd have to answer his questions eventually, but now was not the time.

Colt watched her. "Something important?"

"It's just Blake wanting to know how I'm feeling. I'll tell him I'm feeling super—after we find my dog."

Colt rubbed his knuckles against her low back in support.

Albrecht tapped on his phone until he found the image she asked for. He handed her the device. "Here it is. Ever seen this dude before?"

The man's face struck a chord. She'd seen him some-where. Caitlyn rolled her bottom lip between her teeth and chewed until she remembered. "Colt!" She canted the screen for him to see. "Remember this guy? We saw him the first day of the dog trials."

Colt stared at the photo under scrunched brows. "No. Where was he?"

"In the parking lot! This is the jerk who bumped into me without saying anything, and then he flipped me off. You wanted to kick his ass—remember?" Her pulse surged with renewed strength. "I'm sure it's him!"

"Oh, yeah. That punk with the scraggly beard."

"Yes! I didn't recognize his picture at first because he's clean shaven on his license. But it is definitely him. I know it! And before he ran into me, he got out of a light blue late-model truck! It didn't occur to me before because Berkley said the color of paint was called Indigo Blue Metallic, and I think of Indigo as a dark blue."

"Could he have been targeting us even then?" Colt asked.

"I doubt it." Caitlyn stared at the photo, burning Rankin's image into her mind. "He wouldn't have called attention to himself like that if he was."

Webb slid his phone into his shirt pocket and joined them. "The landlord says after last month's rent never showed up, he came by to collect and found the house abandoned. He had the last month's rent and the security deposit, so he was planning on writing off the loss and re-renting after he had the place cleaned."

"So, we know Rankin's been gone since the first of the month, at least, but he's still in the Phoenix area." Caitlyn frowned. "Let's split up and interview the neighbors. Maybe someone knew Rankin or possibly noticed when he moved out."

Webb pointed east. "We'll take the houses on this side of the block. You two go the other way."

Caitlyn's phone rang. She glanced at the screen and handed it to Colt. "You need to get a new phone."

Colt took the device and sighed before answering. "Allison. What's up?"

∼

"HI, COLT." The saccharine sweetness in her tone made Colt cringe. Allison was clearly up to something. He waited to hear what it was. "I'm just calling to check on Jace."

"You know he's not with me. Why don't you call Dylan or McKenzie?"

"Because I wanted to talk to you. Surely, *you've* been in touch with them."

Colt clamped his teeth together to prevent his exasperation from flying from his mouth in words he'd regret. "Jace is fine and having a fun time with his aunt and uncle. Is that all?"

"Well, no... I have a favor to ask of you."

Of course... here it comes, he thought.

"I wanted to see if we could switch holidays with Jace this year. He's supposed to be with you on Thanksgiving and me for Christmas, but I met someone, and he's invited me to spend Christmas week with him in *Vail*."

A bolt of anger flashed through Colt's chest and heated him even more than the stifling climate in Arizona. "Jace has to come first, Allison. We already have plans for Thanksgiving with the Reeds. It's a big holiday for their family. It's John's favorite, and I don't want to mess things up. He wants to take Jace hunting."

Allison's tone hardened. "First of all, I never approved of Jace going hunting. And second, it's easy for you—you're happily married. But I'm lonely, and I need a life of my own, too. I can't believe you don't understand that."

Colt stopped on the sidewalk, and Caitlyn glanced at him questioningly. He shook his head and held up a finger, mouthing *just a sec.* "I do understand, but we can't jerk Jace around to suit our schedules. It's not fair to him.

He's been looking forward to Thanksgiving with the Reeds."

"You mean changing the plan like you did this past week? He's supposed to be with you, *not* your in-laws."

"Allison, Caitlyn and I were in a car accident in another state. That couldn't be helped. We had *planned* to be home with him."

"Still."

"And it's not like you were at all flexible with me."

"Oh, so this is going to be tit for tat?"

His frustration was building a powerful set of steam, so he pulled in a deep breath and released it in a whoosh. "How about I keep my plans with Jace for Thanksgiving, and if you want to spend Christmas in Vail with your lover, I'll be happy to have Jace for that holiday, too?"

Allison paused, but when she answered, excitement filled the line. "You'd do that? Oh, Colt, that would be fantastic."

What kind of mom would be so pleased to spend the holidays with a new man rather than her own son? "It'll work out better for us anyway, because Logan and his fiancé are getting married at the ranch over Christmas. This way, Jace can be a part of all the family festivities."

"Well, it's all settled then. You'll tell Jace?"

"No, Allison. This news should come from you. Has he met your new boyfriend?"

"Not in that capacity. I'm not ready for that yet."

"Does that mean you haven't told the guy you have a son?"

"I will—when the timing is right. Maybe over

Thanksgiving. Anyway, thanks for keeping Jace for the holidays. Talk to you when you bring him home. Bye!"

Colt met Caitlyn's inquiring gaze. "Looks like we get to have Jace for both holidays this season."

"That's great news." She bent her head so she could see into his down-turned eyes. "So... why don't you look happy about it?"

"I am. It's just that I don't appreciate Allison's attitude. Anyway, let's get back to hunting for Rankin."

"Nothing Allison does should surprise you. But yeah, let's find his ass. He's our only lead to getting Renegade back." Caitlyn knocked on the door of the house next to the abandoned rental.

There was no answer, and Caitlyn peered into the living room window. "No one's home."

The next two houses were the same. They crossed the street and started down the other side. The corner house was empty except for two chihuahuas who leapt onto the back of a sofa under the plate glass and yapped for all they were worth.

Finally, after knocking on the third house on that side of the street, an elderly woman cracked open the entrance and peeked at them from behind a chain that held the door. A waft of coffee scented airconditioned air blasted through the slight opening at them. "Yes?"

Colt held up his badge, even though it was from Wyoming. "Hello, ma'am. I'm Sheriff Colt Branson and this is Deputy US Marshal Caitlyn Reed. We'd like to ask you a few questions about the man who lived across the street."

"Yes?" The woman's expression filled with suspicion.

She did not move to unlock the entrance, so Colt continued speaking through the crack. "Are you acquainted with Melville Rankin?" Colt pointed to Rankin's house. "He lived right over there."

"Mel? Yes, I knew him a little. Nice enough young man. Kept to himself. Why? Is he in trouble?"

"We'd just like to ask him a few questions. Do you know where he is? Or how we can get ahold of him?"

"I don't have any idea where he works, but he gave me his phone number when he first moved in. Will that help?"

"Yes, ma'am. That will do, nicely."

"Wait right there for a minute." The woman closed the door. When she re-opened it, it was without the chain. She handed Colt a scrap of paper. "Here's his number. He wanted me to call if I ever saw anyone poking around. I hope everything is okay. I haven't seen him in a while."

"Everything's fine," Caitlyn reassured her. "How long, exactly, has it been since you last saw Mel?"

"Oh, my goodness, let me see... several weeks, at least. I always knew when he came home because it was usually in the middle of the night and his dogs would bark up a storm."

"Dogs?" Her voice broke on the question.

"Oh, yes. Mel loves dogs. He's always bringing home strays." The old woman's face folded into a web of creases when she smiled.

Colt glanced at Caitlyn, who did not return the woman's grin. In fact, her face had drained of color. She gripped the door frame. "Do you have any idea what

Mel did with the strays? Surely, he didn't keep them all?"

"Oh, no. He only gave them a home until he found someone who wanted to adopt them."

"Like who?"

"I couldn't say. I never met any of them."

Colt pressed his hand against the small of Caitlyn's back to steady her. "Did you ever see any of the new owners? Did they come here to get the dogs?"

"Sometimes," the woman blinked in thought. "But mostly Mel delivered them, I think."

Caitlyn tugged on Colt's arm. "Well, thanks for the phone number. Come on Colt, let's go."

He covered her hand with his, hoping to calm her agitation. "Thank you for your help, ma'am. The police may want to stop by again with further questions. Until then, you've been a lot of help."

The little woman smiled again and adjusted her blouse. "I'm always happy to assist the police."

Colt jogged after Caitlyn, who had practically run down the block toward Webb and Albrecht. "We have Rankin's phone number," she reported when she neared them. "Call in for a warrant to track and search his phone." She thrust the scrap of paper at him. "It sounds like he's got something shady going on with dogs. Hurry!"

14

———

McKenzie peered out the kitchen window when she heard Dylan's truck rumble past the house. He'd gone to pick up Jace after all, since she had to exercise all the dogs. She wiped her hands on a tea towel, grabbed her jacket, and hurried out to greet them.

Jace jumped down from the cab of the huge dually. "Hi, Aunt Kenzie!" He tossed his blond bangs out of his eyes and grinned up at her from underneath his slightly freckled nose.

She gave him a quick hug—the only kind an eleven-year-old boy could tolerate. "Hey, kiddo. We're so glad to have you hang out with us until your dad and Caitlyn come home. Sorry for the change in plans."

"It's okay. Can I go see the dogs?"

Dylan ruffled Jace's hair. "Let's get your backpack put up in your room first. Then you'd better say hello to your grandparents. Grandma Stella will have hurt feelings if you don't eat at least a couple of the cookies she baked for you this morning."

"Cookies? Yes!" Jace took off toward the kitchen door of the big log cabin home.

"Hold it, Mister!" Dylan called after him. "Who do you think is carrying your bag?"

Jace turned around with a shy grin. "Me."

"That's right." Dylan chuckled and tossed the backpack to his nephew.

McKenzie loved seeing her husband interact with the boy, though it made her heart ache. She wanted more than anything to give him a son just like Jace, one day.

It wasn't long before Jace ran out of the kitchen door, letting it slam behind him as he leapt from the stoop. He sped out the gate, wiping cookie crumbs from his mouth as he headed straight for the kennels. "Aunt Kenzie? Can I pet the dogs?"

Before she had a chance to answer, Jace unlatched the first kennel door and slid to his knees in front of Ember, McKenzie's rottweiler—thankfully. She knew her dog was trustworthy around rambunctious kids. Still, what Jace had done was unsafe. "Hey, listen, kiddo. You can't just open the kennel doors and dive in. Sure, Ember is safe and won't run away, but I have several rescue dogs living here right now, and I don't know them well enough to be confident about how they might respond to you."

Jace lifted his face to her with an apologetic grimace that melted into a laughing grin when Ember slurped his cheek with her long, pink tongue. "I'm sorry," he giggled.

"I'm serious, Jace. Some dogs are frightened by children, and they could bite you."

Dylan came up behind her and, taking her shoulders, spoke to their nephew. "Did you hear what Aunt McKenzie said, Jace?"

"Yes, sir." Jace stood but left his hand resting on Ember's broad, square head. "I won't do it again."

"Good." McKenzie reassured him with a smile. "But if you want, I can walk with you and introduce you to all the dogs from outside their gates."

"Yeah!" The exuberant boy returned, leaving no shadow of the contrite one. "Let's go! Bye, Ember. I'll be back later." Jace left Ember's pen, and grabbing hold of McKenzie's arm, he dragged her to the next kennel. "This is Athena. She knows me."

"She sure does. Did you know she is going to have a litter of puppies in about three months?"

"Really? That's so cool! Can I have one?"

McKenzie laughed and shook her head. "No. Her pups will all grow up to be police dogs, like Renegade." The mention of Ren caused a sharp dart to shoot through her chest. She wondered if Caitlyn and Colt had had any luck in finding him yet.

"Sweet!" Jace was off to the next kennel where the gray pit bull she'd nick-named Storm lay curled up in the back corner of his pen.

"Be careful with this dog, Jace. He was aggressive with some other dogs in town, and Doctor Moore asked me to watch him for a couple of days. He could be dangerous."

Jace nodded and stared at the dog. The dog stared back with sad eyes. McKenzie held her breath. Her nephew dropped to his knees. "Hi, boy. Are you scared? Don't be afraid. I won't hurt you."

Storm's eyes did not waiver from Jace. Finally, his tail wiggled once, but then he rested his muzzle on the ground between his front paws.

"It's okay, boy." Without looking at McKenzie, he asked, "What's his name?"

"I'm not sure, so I've been calling him Storm."

"Storm," he said, rolling the word out across his tongue. "I like that. Hey, Storm, buddy. You're safe here. Okay?"

"Want to see the other dogs?" McKenzie asked.

"Can I just sit here for a while?"

Her heart warmed. "Of course. But no fingers through the fence, okay?"

"Okay."

"Promise?" McKenzie wanted to be sure he heard her.

"I promise."

She moved down the kennel row, checking to be sure all the dogs had eaten their breakfasts and made certain their waters were full. She was at the end of the row when she heard the clang of a gate behind her. Her stomach dropped. *Jace!*

McKenzie screamed, "Jace!" and raced back to Storm's kennel. Her agitation caused all the dogs to bark, and Dylan ran out from the barn. "Jace!" She called again. Her heart pounded as she ran to the pit bull's gate, terrified at what she might find.

She quickly realized there was no need for panic. Curled up on the dog bed were both Jace and Storm. The gray dog bathed Jace's hands, no doubt tasting cookie remnants, as the boy lay against his muscled shoulder.

"Jace, what are you doing in there? You scared me to

death!" McKenzie opened the gate while she caught her breath. "I'm glad you two are getting along, but it could have gone much differently. He could have hurt you badly. You broke your promise and disobeyed me. Now, come out of there, this instant."

Dylan murmured behind her. "When I was a kid, my dad would have given me a serious woopin' for something like this."

"Well, Jace is not our kid. And he's not getting a *woopin'*. But there will be a consequence." She raised her voice, "Jace, instead of going fishing with your uncle this morning, you'll be spending the next few hours cleaning out all the dog kennels."

A look of incredulity filled his face. "But Uncle Dylan promised we could go!"

"Well, you promised me you wouldn't open the kennels, too. You broke your word. Storm could have seriously injured you."

"But he didn't! Storm likes me!" Earnestness radiated from his eyes as he slung an arm around the dog's neck.

It was true. It seemed there was an instant bond between the dog and the boy. But Jace had to learn to mind the rules on the ranch. "I can see that. And I'm glad, but you still broke your word. Come on out of there, and I'll show you where the pooper scooper is."

Dylan kissed her cheek and whispered. "I didn't do anything wrong. Why am I getting punished?"

His beard tickled her ear, and she shrugged her shoulder against him. "Because you are going to be a good example to Jace and back me up."

"Boy, I can see our kids are gonna have to learn to behave if I ever want to go fishing."

"That's right. They will." The image of her favorite dream of camping with Dylan and three little people that looked just like him had her grinning. She hooked her arm around his neck and pulled him close for a kiss. "And I can't wait."

15

———————

Detective Webb thanked whomever he spoke with on the phone and ended the call. "We should have our warrant in about an hour."

"An hour?" Caitlyn's skin itched with impatience. "Why so long?"

"It's lunchtime, and since we don't need the warrant to save anyone's life, they'll get to it when they feel like it. It could be sooner. You never know."

"It might save my partner's life. Did you tell them that?" She hated feeling out of control. The doctor mentioned something about having these sorts of feelings and she couldn't tell if her frustration came from her head injury or was legitimate.

Colt massaged the bunched muscles in her neck and shoulders. "Speaking of lunch, why don't we grab some food while we're waiting?"

Albrecht clapped his hands together. "Now you're talking. I'm starving. Let's grab a burger, then as soon as we hear from the judge, we'll track the bastard down. Can't work on an empty stomach."

"Fine, but if we get the call, we're going whether we've eaten or not." Caitlyn directed the words to Colt, but she intended them to them all.

"We will, Catie. Everyone understands how important this is."

She disagreed. Otherwise, Webb would have explained to the judge how urgent the warrant was.

They all climbed into their cars, and Colt followed Albrecht to a nearby burger shop. They went inside, and Caitlyn's stomach made a triple-axel flip when she smelled French fries cooking. She'd been fighting fatigue all morning, but she didn't realize how hungry she was. The last time she'd eaten anything was when she'd had the ice cream Colt brought to her at the hospital. Begrudgingly, she admitted to herself that food was necessary if she wanted to find Renegade.

She stepped up to the counter, and staring at the menu hanging from the ceiling, she ordered. "I'll have the double patty with all the fixings, large fries, and chocolate shake." Colt chuckled under his breath, so she elbowed his ribs. "Shut up. I'm hungry and since we're here…" Her abdomen seized in a deep cramp, and she sucked in a breath and held it until the pain receded hoping Colt didn't notice.

"Glad to see you've got your appetite back." His handsome smile soothed something inside her and made her want to bury her head in his chest and lean on his strength. Instead, she squared her shoulders, opting to use her own grit to face her problems.

Colt ordered next, and they joined the detectives at a table by the window to wait for both their food and the warrant.

The call came when Caitlyn was halfway through her burger. She wiped a juicy mustard drip from her chin. As soon as she heard Webb say he'd received the electronic document on his phone, she dropped her sandwich, pushed her chair out, and stood. Colt took her hand and pulled her back down to her seat. "Finish your food. We have the warrant, but it will still take some time to track the phone."

Webb agreed. "Another half hour or so to track or triangulate the location. Hang in there, Deputy Marshal. We'll have the information as soon as the tech team can get it to us."

Caitlyn recognized the understanding in his eyes and was grateful it came without pity. This wasn't about her. It was about finding Renegade.

"Yeah," Albrecht piped in. "We get it. We'd feel the same way if it was our partner who was missing."

Caitlyn settled back into her seat. "Thanks, guys." She appreciated their support, but her edgy energy remained, ping-ponging along her nerves.

When they finished eating, Albrecht wanted a smoke, so they waited for him by their cars. The second call came, and the stout detective stamped out the butt on the street.

"This is Webb." The senior detective listened to the caller. "I understand. We'll go have a look. Thanks for the rush." He dropped his phone into his shirt pocket. "They couldn't get us the exact whereabouts without a call being made to or from his cell, but they triangulated the location with the device's internal identity number and using the coordinates of his last call."

"Great! Let's go." Caitlyn jerked open her car door.

"We will, but you need to understand, the location is way out in the desert, and the tracking is less reliable there. Rural towers are much farther apart than they are in the city, so we have square miles to search rather than just a few city blocks."

Refusing to be discouraged, Caitlyn let out a puff of air. "But you have greater visibility across the distance in a rural environment."

Webb glanced up at the sun as he mopped sweat from the back of his neck. "I suppose, but there are dangers out in the desert."

"All the more reason to find my dog." Caitlyn tilted her chin upward, ready to shut down any argument for waiting until it got cooler. No one challenged her.

Colt and Caitlyn climbed into their rental and headed out of town. Webb and Albrecht followed them. The two cars drove over forty-five minutes before they came to the location of the first cell tower. It seemed as though nothing living ventured out there in the heat of the day—not even any birds. Colt crested a hill that dropped into a slight valley between dunes.

"With their arms, the cactus here looks like the kind you see in cartoons," Caitlyn observed, wishing there were more of them to see.

"They're called Saguaro cacti."

"How do you know that?"

Colt grinned. "I know all sorts of incredibly valuable information."

"Hmmm." Caitlyn smirked and then propped her elbow on the armrest and rested her chin in her hand. Her gaze scanned the barren land. She glimpsed a slight movement in the distance, so she sat up and squinted for a better view.

"Do you see something?" Colt reached behind her seat and rummaged, one-handed, in his bag. He pulled out a pair of binoculars and passed them to her.

"Thanks." Caitlyn held them to her eyes and tried to find the object that had caught her attention. "I don't see anything anymore. It was probably a mirage."

She rested the lenses in her lap but kept scanning the random desert scrub. "Wait! It's back." She pointed and peered through the binoculars once again. "Something is flashing in the sun, but I can't make out what it is."

Colt found a road that led in the general direction of the glinting object and drove across the packed sand towards its location. As they got closer, they saw a predator fence surrounding a five-acre property. Plastic signs printed with black lightning bolts warned viewers to STAY OUT—ELECTRIC FENCE.

Colt slowed, and they rolled past an electric gate. Up the dirt driveway beyond the entrance sat a mobile home that had lived a long, hard life. It was probably once white, but now wore a belt of rust where trim used to be. The owner put up a wooden privacy fence behind the trailer that formed a yard taking up at least two acres on the back side of the property. They saw no cars parked anywhere, but that didn't necessarily mean no one was there.

Caitlyn rolled her lower lip in between her teeth and bit down in thought. "Why do you suppose there is such an intense security fence surrounding such a sad little house?"

"It's a good question, and my first guess is drugs."

"Probably. Drive around back."

Caitlyn's phone rang. It was Webb. "This place is owned by a man named Cal Riggs."

"Any record?"

"Yeah. A death record. Guy died four years ago."

"Interesting. What did Riggs do for a living before he died?"

"Looks like he lived off the government teat. No other obvious income. I'll look into it further."

"Which one of you boys wants to pee on the fence to see if it's live?" she teased.

"I nominate Albrecht. He already has a passel of kids." Webb went silent, then cleared his throat. "Uh, sorry. Bad joke."

"No need to pussyfoot around me, Webb. It's no big deal." Caitlyn looked away as she breathed through the sudden ache his off-handed comment had caused.

Web moved on. "What do you guys think is behind that wood fence?"

"Something worth hiding. There are no neighbors to want privacy from." They drove past the end of the tall barricade. On the property beyond the yard lay a dingy white pit bull-cross with a brown spot that covered one ear. He lay in the dust but jumped to his feet, barking, when he saw their car. His ribs stood out like a ship's hull, and he wore a thick chain collar attached to another chain heavy enough to pull a car. There was no shelter to protect him from the sweltering heat of the sun.

"Oh, my God. Colt. Pull over." When he did, she jumped from the car.

"Don't get too near that fence, Catie."

Webb stopped his car behind Colt's, and both detectives got out and watched Caitlyn.

"I won't," she called. "But look at that poor dog. What is he chained to?"

Albrecht stepped closer. "Looks almost like a truck axle."

At the back of the property stood a makeshift shed. Caitlyn walked as close to it as she could. Inside the lean-to, there was a ten-by-two-inch plank bolted across the center of the shack. It had heavy hooks screwed into it, each about a foot apart. The board hung approximately five feet in the air.

Next to the plank was a contraption that resembled a head catch for cows, only much smaller. Snugged up against the side of the shed was an apparatus that looked to Caitlyn like a rickety wooden treadmill from the 1930s. When she saw it, her blood iced over, making her shiver even in the hundred degree-plus temperature. "Colt!" she screamed. "We have to get inside this property. Now!"

y the time Blake called for a late checkout and ordered brunch, it was after eleven. A knock sounded, and Blake pulled on his crumpled dress shirt and jockeys before he padded over to answer it. Their food had arrived. He opened the door wide and stood out of the way.

The server wheeled their meal in on a linen covered tray. He lifted silver domes off a platter of fluffy scrambled eggs, a plate mounded with crispy bacon, and another stacked high with steaming pancakes. The blended aromas sent rumbles through Blake's stomach.

"Orange juice in the carafe, and coffee for two in the thermos, sir. Is there anything else I can get for either of you?"

"No, thanks. This looks great. I'm starving."

The young man looked away, but not before Blake saw his mouth twitch and the glint of humor in his eye. Blake grinned. It had been a long time since he'd woken with such an appetite. He reached for his wallet, and following the bellhop to the exit, he tipped him generously in sync with his elevated mood. As soon as the kid left, Blake threw the dead bolt.

Once he locked the door, Allison released the fierce grip she'd had on the sheet she'd been holding over her chest. "We will never eat all this food."

"Speak for yourself. I'm diving headfirst into those eggs." Blake poured them each a cup of coffee and dribbled cream into his.

He filled his dish with the steaming scramble, while Allison added cream and three spoons of sugar to her coffee. She sipped her sweet concoction while she watched him eat. He finished his eggs and five strips of salty bacon before lifting two pancakes from the pile onto his plate.

"Want syrup?" Allison tilted the small pitcher but instead of pouring it on his cakes, she slowly drizzled a long, swirling line across her bare abdomen up to her breastbone.

Blake's heart flip-flopped. "I *do* love maple syrup." He set his pancakes aside.

LATER, when he was drying off from his shower, Blake heard Allison on the phone. He took his time brushing his teeth to give her some privacy. When she finished with her call, he slid on the complimentary hotel robe and rejoined the messy-haired beauty in the bed.

"Everything okay?" He lifted a strawberry from their breakfast tray and fed it to her.

Catching a drop of juice in her palm, she smiled. "I was just making arrangements for the holidays."

"What kind of arrangements? Do you have a pet who needs watching or something?"

"Or something."

"I'm so happy you're coming with me. Now, I'm looking forward to Christmas." He nuzzled her neck. "Do you ski?"

"No, but I don't mind shopping and waiting by the fire at the lodge while you do."

"You could take a lesson."

"I'd rather sit by the fireplace drinking wine and reading magazines. I can sleep in, maybe get a massage..."

"Sounds like you've done this before." He lifted her fingers and kissed each knuckle.

She pulled her hand back and pouted her full lips. "Speaking of doing things before... last night was so... well, so incredible. Except..."

"Except, what?" He propped himself on his elbow and regarded her, preparing his ego for whatever blow was about to hit him. Had he bored her?

"I didn't say anything at the time, but... well..." She raised her chin and sniffed. "At one particularly exciting moment, you called out *Caitlyn's* name."

"No. No way." The blood drained from his head as he shook it. Her accusation kicked him hard in the gut. Had he really made such a blunder? There was that period of time during round three when he had been fantasizing, but no way did he say Caitlyn's name out loud. *Christ.* Blake did his best to keep his expression neutral. "Why would I do something like that when *your* name is the only one that's been on my mind since we met?"

"Well, I wasn't hearing things." Her voice hardened. "You hardly ever say my name, so I think I'd know if you called out a name that *wasn't* Allison."

He sat up and caressed her shoulder. "I'm not sure what you heard, but I didn't say another woman's name. I wouldn't."

Her gaze fell to her lap, and her lips flattened with a sigh. "It's okay if you did—I guess. I understand. Believe me, I know what it's like not being able to get over someone. I had heard you and Caitlyn Reed were involved awhile back. I just didn't realize how intimate you had been."

He wished he and Caitlyn *had* been intimate, but they didn't have a chance before Branson pushed his way into things. "Allison let's not talk about any of that. It's in the past. All I want to do is spend the rest of the time we have left in our room enjoying each other." He kissed her until she relaxed and had hopefully let him off the hook.

She slid his robe from his shoulders. "I guess you'll have to work extra hard to convince me *I'm* the one you want to take with you to Vail. Maybe you can prove it to me over Thanksgiving. Got any plans?"

"What do you have in mind?"

"I just found out that I'm free the entire four-day weekend. How about we sneak away to somewhere nice, like Jackson Hole?"

Blake grinned. This woman was going to be expensive, but if she wanted to keep him company over the long, lonely holiday season, and if she could help him get over Caitlyn Reed, she would be worth every cent.

17

To support McKenzie's disciplinary action with Jace, Stella switched the plan from lunch to dinner. Which was fine. She preferred to cook an evening meal over a campfire, anyway, and this late in the autumn they would appreciate the heat. If the fishers were lucky, they might provide some trout for supper, but just in case they weren't so fortunate, she packed the ingredients for Hobo Stew.

Since theirs was a cattle ranch, the Reeds always had plenty of beef, and Stella took three packs of meat from the freezer. She added potatoes, onions, mushrooms, a jar of green beans, a can of miniature corn, and a couple of red peppers to the food hamper. Knowing that everyone had different preferences, she packed barbeque, soy, teriyaki, and steak sauces to season the individual stew packets with. For dessert, she'd make upside-down chocolate-cherry cake in her cast-iron Dutch oven.

John strode into the kitchen and peered into her basket. "Got my bourbon in there?" He reached for a cookie from a plate on the counter, ducking to miss the dishcloth Stella snapped at him.

"Those cookies are for Jace, and you can carry your own bourbon." Laughing, Stella shooed him away from the food.

"But you'll be driving in the truck. I'm riding my horse." John spun around the counter and snatched another cookie.

"Then carry a flask." She sent him a mock glare. "Speaking of riding, are you and Dylan comfortable with Jace handling Whiskey by himself all the way to the river?"

"Come on, Stell, he's ten years old. Our kids were riding their own horses by the time they were four. Besides, he does just fine with him in the arena, and Whiskey is as solid as the day is long." John bit into the chocolate chip. "Of course, that's if the kid can stay out of trouble long enough that we get to go. Who ever heard of starting a fishing trip after lunch?"

"Oh, stop your complaining. The point is teaching him how to fish, not how to catch."

"Well, catching is the fun part." He reached for Stella and caught her around the waist. A laugh bubbled up her throat. "See?" He drew her close and tasting of cookies, he kissed her. Gently at first, but soon the heat rose.

Stella brushed her fingers along the short silver taper of hair at his temples and threaded them up into the longer strands. He pulled her tight against him and deepened the kiss. She would have never believed they would find their passion again, but something about the Irish countryside, or simply being away from the ranch and all its responsibilities, had lit their fire once more.

The back door slammed open, and Stella jumped like a teenager caught necking in a movie theater. Dylan stood in the doorway, gaping at them. He soon recovered his wit. "Get a room, you two. For crying out loud, there is a child running around this place."

"We have a room. It's called the kitchen," John grumbled.

"Can't you take it elsewhere? Our food is made in here!"

Stella's cheeks burned, but John chuckled. "Hasn't hurt you so far."

"Oh, God. Dad! Come on!" Dylan grimaced.

McKenzie came through the door after Dylan, with Jace in tow. "What's going on? What'd we miss?"

Stella took charge before the men in her life could embarrass her further. "Not a thing. These two hooligans were just getting out of my kitchen, so I can finish packing the food for our trip. Are you all set?"

"Almost. Jace brought a jacket, but I don't think it'll be warm enough after the sun goes down. I wondered if there was something here he could borrow? And he'll need a hat and gloves, too."

"Check Caitlyn's old room. She might have left an old coat in there. It will be too big, but it'll be the smallest we have. He can borrow a hat and gloves from me. They're in the hall closet."

"Thanks!" McKenzie left to collect the items she wanted.

Dylan called after her, "Don't baby the kid. The best way to learn to have the right gear is to not have it once."

"You would know," John teased.

Stella held her breath, hoping Dylan heard the joking tone in his father's voice. It would be just like the two of them to turn something like this into an argument.

Dylan's eyes narrowed slightly, but then he grinned. "That is *exactly* how I learned. Remember that camping trip you took me, Logan, and Colt on?" He turned to include Stella in the story. "It was January, and Dad thought we needed to learn cold weather survival. I wore my cowboy hat and forgot to bring a knit cap to keep my ears warm. I'm surprised I still have earlobes!"

With a twinkle in his eye, John picked up the tale. "You had to sleep with a sweater wrapped around your head, so you wouldn't freeze to death."

"That's right. Well, I never forgot any of my winter gear again. I can tell you that."

"You two." Stella's heart was full seeing her son and husband enjoying a memory together. "Don't be too hard on Jace. He is new to ranch and mountain life, and I doubt his mother helped him pack. Give him a while before you force him to learn the hard way. Besides, shouldn't Colt be the one to decide how his son should learn those things?"

"Not if he's gonna be a member of *this* family." John pulled her close again. "He'll have to cowboy-up sometime, and the sooner the better." He brushed the base of her neck with his lips and kissed his way up.

"Come on, Dad! Seriously!" Dylan complained, but

he chuckled as he walked out of the kitchen and left John to his antics.

"You shoo, John. Go on and get ready to go. We're already getting a late start."

"I'm all set. Just have to get the horses tacked up. Is McKenzie riding a horse, or will she come along in the truck with you?"

"Since Jace will be on Whiskey, I think she's coming with me." Stella packed a jar of cherry pie filling and a cake mix in the bag. "Will you carry this out for me?"

18

"What's wrong? What do you see?" Colt called. The urgency in Caitlyn's voice had sent adrenaline surging through his veins. He left the engine running and jumped out to join her.

"I think this is a place where some asshole keeps dogs for fighting."

"What makes you believe that? I only see one dog."

Caitlyn dashed over to Webb's car. The sudden movement and the hot sun caused her head to pound. She pressed her fingertips against her closed eyelids. Albrecht rolled down his window. "What's going on?"

She breathed through the pain. "I'm pretty sure this is a breeding and training compound for dog fighting. I'm going to call my brother, who is a K9 agent with the FBI. He'll know what to look for. Then, if I'm right, we can call for another warrant that allows us to enter this property forcibly.

The detectives looked past Caitlyn with confused expressions that mimicked the one Colt was sure covered his own face. Maybe Caitlyn was overreacting to seeing the dog chained like he was. She'd been under a tremendous amount of stress. "Catie, sweetheart…"

She spun around and had to grip the car to keep her balance. Her face was pale as she glared at him, and she tapped on her phone. "Don't 'Catie, sweetheart' me! Listen to me, Colt. I'll bet my career that dog is being used for fighting and that there are more dogs hidden behind that privacy fence."

She described what she saw to Logan and listened to his reply. "Okay, so I'm not out of my mind." She sent Colt a look that screamed, *I told you so*! "What else should I be looking for?"

"I can't get any closer. They have the place surrounded by a five-foot electric fence." She paused for her brother's comments. "I never thought of that. But we'd still need a warrant, and it's a chicken and egg situation. I need to get inside to see if there's enough evidence to merit calling a judge for a warrant to get inside. I'll call you back when I know anything."

The sickly dog on the chain barked and snarled at Caitlyn, lunging in her direction until his chain jerked him back. His barks elicited others from behind the fence.

"Do you hear that?" Colt pointed toward the wooden fence.

"More dogs! I knew it! With any luck, Webb will get ahold of a dog-loving judge."

Webb climbed out of his car and approached. "Already on it. Now, tell me exactly what you see that makes you suspect dog fighting."

Webb repeated, word for word, what Caitlyn described in the shed and the condition of the dog that was chained by itself outside in the heat without shelter. Webb thanked the person on the call. "We should hear within a half hour. If we're lucky, and we get a judge with a heart for animals, we'll get a call even sooner. I'm calling for SWAT backup either way, so we'll be ready to breach if we get the go ahead."

Colt cupped Caitlyn's shoulders. "Do you think Renegade is in there?"

"I don't know, but I'm not leaving here until I find out."

"What did Logan say?"

"He agreed that the apparatus I saw in the shed is most likely a treadmill used for exercising dogs. I guess they give dogs hormones to bulk them up and then run them to build muscle. The miniature head-catcher is used to trap female dogs and force them into breeding. Logan said those items and the condition of the pit bull mix were solid indicators of a dog fighting operation."

"What about that board with the hooks?"

She swallowed hard before answering. "Apparently, that is where they hang dogs that don't perform well enough in the fighting ring."

"No." Colt shook his head, and his stomach knotted up. Who could do something like that to a dog?

"Yes." She let out a long breath. "Logan also told me

how to short circuit the electric fence if I wanted to." Her mouth curled into a small smile, but there was no joy or humor in her eyes. "And I'll do that if we can't get a warrant."

"You'd break in?"

"Damn straight. We might not get our day in court, but we would save the lives of those dogs."

"And get arrested in the process."

"I don't care. If Renegade is in there, nothing is stopping me from getting to him." Angry tears glistened in her eyes.

"We'll find him, Catie. I know we will."

She nodded and leaned against his chest. "Or die trying."

Webb and Albrecht joined them at the fence. The tall detective held up his phone. A warrant document filled the screen. "We got it, and SWAT will be here any minute."

"I'm not waiting for them. Colt, Renegade's kennel and pad are in the trunk of the car, right?"

"Yeah..." Wariness prickled his skin. What was his impetuous wife up to this time?

"Help me get his pad out." She ran to the car. Colt popped the trunk open with the fob and they tugged out the thick rectangular cushion.

"What are you planning to do with this?" He held onto the cushion so she couldn't run off without answering.

"Logan said I could drape a heavy blanket or something like that over the fence to gain access. Since we have a warrant, I'm going to use this. I'll need you to boost me."

"No way am I letting you go in there alone."

"Then have Webb and Albrecht boost you over, too. Come on!" She tugged the pad out of his hands and flopped it over the electrified mesh that was almost as tall as she was.

"Are you armed?" Colt asked as he cupped his hands for her foot.

"Always." Caitlyn patted her holster out of habit before she placed her hands on the pad and sprang from his lift, swinging her legs to the side. She cleared the humming fence with ease. But crouched to the ground, holding her head on the other side.

Webb boosted Colt, and he followed her over. "Is your head okay? I think you should wait in the car."

"I'm fine. Let's go." Caitlyn got to her feet and strode toward the interior fence.

The detective cautioned them. "Just get a look at what's on the other side of the privacy fence. That's it. Do not attempt to gain entry without backup. Is that clear?"

Colt gave him a thumbs up, knowing he couldn't vouch that his wife would follow Webb's rules. Not if there was even a slight chance that Renegade was there.

Together, Colt and Caitlyn ran for cover behind the slatted wood, avoiding getting too close to the dog on the chain. Colt boosted Caitlyn up again. This time, he held her steady while she peered over the top of the barrier. Her body stilled.

"Oh, my God, Colt. Let me down."

Her face was white, and she covered her nose and mouth with her hand, pulling it slightly away so she could speak. "There are lots of dogs back there and the ground is covered in dog poop baking in the heat. She jutted her chin forward. "I'm calling the local ASPCA."

19

"American Society for the Prevention of Cruelty to Animals. How can I help you?" A woman's soft voice answered Caitlyn's call.

"Hello. This is Deputy US Marshal Caitlyn Reed. We've just come upon a property in the desert outside of Phoenix that is being used for breeding and training dogs to fight. There are approximately twenty-five dogs behind the fence that I can see. There might be more." At first look, she did not see Renegade among the dogs chained in the over-sized yard. Maybe he was inside the trailer. She couldn't bear any other possibilities—she could only hope and wait for SWAT to show up so they could breach the compound.

"Oh, dear." The woman sounded as sick as Caitlyn felt.

"All the dogs I've seen are too thin—even the ones obviously jacked up on muscle building steroids. Many are licking scabs from cuts and bites. Their wounds are festering with flies."

Caitlyn glanced up at Colt who, after hearing her description, hoisted himself up on the fence to see for himself. His biceps trembled before he let himself back down, and the horror of what he saw shadowed his eyes.

She told her lungs to keep breathing. Getting the help these dogs needed was the first step. Her heart ached at the idea of Renegade facing these conditions. Being made to live like this. Forced to fight. She pushed the images from her mind and refused to allow them to distract her. At that moment, she had to do everything she could to rescue those animals immediately.

"Yes, it's common for these dogs to be dosed with performance-enhancing drugs used to increase their fighting potential and to keep injured dogs fighting longer." The woman from ASPCA sighed. "I'll call our team together." Caitlyn shuddered at the information, and the woman cleared her throat. "If you'll give me the address, we'll get there as soon as we can. Please, keep everyone away from the animals until we can assess them. They could be extremely dangerous. We can't know what all they've suffered through."

"I will." Caitlyn read her the address of the property. "And thank you." She ended the call.

The sound of sirens jolted her into considering their next step—breaching the trailer and the yard behind it. If Ren was in there somewhere, she'd find him.

The massive, tactical gun-metal gray SWAT vehicle skidded to a stop at the entrance to the electric fence. The team captain called out on loudspeakers to anyone inside the mobile home or on the property to show themselves and to open the gate. There was no human movement, but the loud noise scared the dogs, who howled and barked in response.

After a second warning, when no one surfaced, the SWAT team poured from the back door wearing helmets and urban armor. They followed their vehicle into the property as it rammed through the gate, sending metal railings, fence pieces, and sparks flying as though the barricade was made of balsa wood.

Their choreographed movements were like a military ballet. They communicated using hand motions as half the team approached the front door. Two smaller groups split off to the sides. A cop carrying a battering ram ran to the entrance. It only took one hit for the flimsy door to collapse under the swing.

SWAT members entered the small structure, each covering the other as they went. Caitlyn heard the word "clear" shouted four times, before they announced, "All clear." At that point, it was safe for the other cops to canvas the rest of the property. Caitlyn had clipped her badge to her belt and followed them into the fenced-off area.

She ran through the acreage filled with chained-up, half-starved and abused dogs, dodging stinking piles of feces. Her heart breaking for them as she raced to find Renegade. She screamed his name until her voice broke in the dry Arizona air. All the dogs chained to the cracked dirt looked to be pit bulls or pit mixes. Whoever imprisoned them kept the dogs far enough apart from each other to avoid contact, but close enough to encourage fighting over food and drink. Most had no shelter, and those that did still suffered from heat, biting flies, and a lack of water. So far, she saw no Belgian Malinois.

A very pregnant bitch strained to reach a water bowl that was a foot outside of her reach. Caitlyn nudged the container closer so she could get a drink but didn't dare approach her. She'd leave that to the people who knew how to help damaged dogs like these. She had massive respect for the employees and volunteers who worked for the ASPCA.

A lone, wilting shed at the far end of the yard was the only place left she had yet to look for Renegade. Her pulse rocketed as she walked toward the shack. As she got near, she smelled the sickening-sweet odor of decay. Her throat contracted, and her head shook from side to side as if her brain was telling her to stop—not to go any closer. Not to open the door.

Still, she forced her feet to move. Step by step, she steeled herself for what she might see inside. Hundreds of flies buzzed around the cracks of the flimsy structure.

Colt yelled to her from across the yard, "Catie! No! Don't go in there. Wait for me!" His racing footfalls pounded the dusty ground behind her, but she took another step forward and reached for the latch. The stench forced her to pinch her nose and cover her mouth with her left hand. Tears blurred her vision. Swallowing hard, she pulled open the door.

The plywood dropped off its hinges and a cloud of hot, putrefying air, thick with flies, blasted out at her. She shoved the broken wood away and batted at the bugs surrounding her head. She stepped back, coughing. Colt reached her side, and he yanked her away from the opening and she vomited, spitting the acrid bile onto the dirt.

"Good God." He pressed his nose against his forearm. "Catie, stay over here. Let me look inside." He physically pushed her backward several more steps to where the air was breathable. She didn't resist because her head felt woozy, and her knees wobbled. Instead, she watched the man she loved make the sacrifice of looking at whatever horror lay within.

Obviously shaken, Colt backed slowly out of the shack. Tears hovered in his eyes when he turned to her. "Don't go in there, Catie." Colt's gag reflex kicked in. He bent over and braced his hands on his knees, but he managed not to puke.

Caitlyn tried to push past him, but he grabbed her and held her fast. "Trust me. You don't want that image in your head."

"Colt, let go of me!" She jerked away from his grasp and lunged toward the open door.

He caught up to her in two giant strides. Gripping her arms, he held her back, keeping her from seeing the abomination inside the shed. "Renegade's not in there." Caitlyn started crying and her knees gave way. Colt caught her before she collapsed on the ground. "It's not him, Catie. Did you hear me?"

She could only nod. Relief flooded her nervous system. She felt thankful that Ren had escaped being one of the helpless animals that someone had used, abused, and thrown into the shack to rot. But her heart bled for the poor dogs who were. Caitlyn clung to Colt until she regained some of her strength.

Detective Webb joined them. "The kitchen cupboards are filled with steroids and dog food. It doesn't look like anyone lives here. There's no food or clothing anywhere, though there is a dingy bed in one of the back rooms. I think this place is probably used as a crash pad for whoever is keeping the dogs."

"Deputy Marshal Reed?" A SWAT Officer leapt from the back deck of the trailer. "Ma'am, we found a stack of fliers on the kitchen table." He thrust a handful of hand-made advertisements for a local dog fight.

She scanned the text. "This event is happening tonight!" She read the paper more carefully and then flipped it over to see if there was any more information on the back side. "It says when the fights are, but not where. How will we find them?"

20

McKenzie sat shotgun beside Stella in John's truck on the way up to the Reeds' favorite family fishing hole along the portion of Moose Creek that meandered through the ranch property. The men and boy on horseback took a mountain trail. John led the way and Dylan followed Jace, who rode Caitlyn's horse. When they got to the river, Stella pulled the truck off to the side, leaving plenty of room for all the fishing gear and a campfire.

The women unpacked everything from the cab while they waited for the cowboys to catch up. The boys were laughing at some, most likely off-color, joke when their horses trotted into camp.

"Having fun?" McKenzie asked Jace.

His eyes were alight with wonder. "Aunt Kenzie! Grandpa had to shoot a rattler right from the back of his horse!! It was *awesome!*"

She blinked, looking first at John, who showed no remorse, and then at her husband who, though he had the discipline not to allow his mouth to smile, couldn't hide the merriment in his eyes. She grumbled, "I'm not sure that was something you should do in front of a child."

John snickered. "Better than letting his horse get bit and bucking him off."

"Well..." McKenzie sputtered. "Still."

Dylan dismounted. "It's part of life up here, Kenze. And you can see Jace is no worse for seeing it."

"It was so cool!" Jace jumped down from his saddle. "Blood and pieces of snake flew everywhere!"

She scowled in disgust at that, and both men laughed. Dylan took his horse, Sampson, with Whiskey and tied them to a tree. When he returned, he pulled McKenzie into his arms and whispered in her ear. "See? He's fine. Boys like that kind of thing." He drew back and scratched his bearded chin. "Boys and Caitlyn, that is."

"Never mind." McKenzie wondered if she would ever get fully used to living a ranch life. If they had kids, Dylan would inevitably teach them all of it, whether she understood it or not. "Stella and I put your fishing tackle over by that big log. You guys better get started if we're going to have any trout for dinner." She winked at Dylan and went to help Stella prepare the food she brought just in case they had no luck with fish.

After she and Stella started a fire and finished prepping the dinner, they sat on the log next to the river. The water rippled lazily over rocks beneath the surface, and Stella knitted while they watched their men teach Jace how to bait his hook and cast his line. John and Dylan wore waders and used fly rods, but since this was Jace's first time, he stood on the edge of the water and learned by using a kid-sized rod and reel.

"Hey, little man. You've got to let your worm sit in the water for longer than two seconds." Dylan waded his way to Jace on the bank. "You want your bait to look like something a fish wants to eat. The trout will watch it for a few seconds before it tries to eat it. If you yank it out of the water too soon, you'll never get a bite."

Jace nodded sagely as though he'd just heard the world's greatest wisdom. Dylan made his way back to into the river, and Jace reached into a small plastic tub of worms. He pulled out a fat one to re-bait his hook.

A second later, he cried out, thrusting his hand into the air. "The hook is in my hand!" he screamed. "Get it out!"

McKenzie shot to her feet in panic, but Dylan merely glanced over his shoulder. John kept fishing. "I'm coming, Jace," she cried. "Don't move!" She ran to the boy's side.

By the time she got there, Dylan had already made his unhurried way to his nephew. He held Jace's hand and peered up at her. "Don't worry, Kenze. My mom's a pro at getting hooks out of fingers."

"What? How many hooks does one have to remove from someone's flesh to become a professional? What are we going to tell Colt?" McKenzie wondered if Colt would ever trust them to watch his son again. What kind of parents would she and Dylan make? Obviously, the kind who put their kids in danger.

"McKenzie?" Dylan's voice broke through her panicked thoughts. "Can you please get my mom?" His voice was as calm as the sleepy river they fished in. How could he be so blasé?

"Yes...right." She turned and ran back to the picnic set up. Her mother-in-law was bent into the cab of the truck, searching for something. "Stella! Stella!" McKenzie dashed over to the older woman and tugged on her arm.

"What is it? What's happened?" Stella's eyes bulged with fear as she pushed past McKenzie and hurried to the river's edge.

"It's no big deal, mom," Dylan said. Jace caught himself instead of a fish. Can you help him get this hook out of his finger?"

Stella's shoulders relaxed by several inches, and she covered her heart with her hand. "Oh, for heaven's sake. By the tone in McKenzie's voice, I thought someone had drowned." She sent a kind and encouraging smile to Jace. "Come on out of there, young man. Let's take that hook out and get you back to fishing. How does that sound?" She reached out a hand to help stabilize the boy as he climbed up the bank to level ground. His eyes darted with uncertainty between Dylan, Stella, and McKenzie.

Dylan called out to him, "Don't worry, buddy. Grandma Stella can get that barb out of you without you feeling anything. You'll be fine." His gaze slid to McKenzie. "I promise. He's fine."

She felt foolish being the only Reed to react so strongly and followed Stella to the truck to see exactly what magic the woman knew.

Stella had a pot of water already heating on the campfire. "Here, Jace. This water is warm, and we'll use it to wash your hands. Then I'm going to put some ice from the cooler on the place you've hooked. As soon as it's good and numb, I'll pop that hook out, and you'll be right as rain. How does that sound?"

Jace nodded, but his eyes held fear when he looked at McKenzie. She smiled with as much confidence as she could muster, and Jace responded by thrusting his wounded hand toward Stella. It was an amazing feeling —lending a child the courage he needed to be brave. Was that why the Reeds had all been so calm?

Once Stella deemed the area on Jace's finger was numb enough, she cut the tail of the fishing line that remained in the hook's eye and used it to loop around its curve. She gave it a firm tug, and out it came. Jace stared at his hand and then blinked up at his grandma.

Stella smiled softly and stroked his cheek. "You were very brave, Jace. I'm proud of you. Now, let me put some anti-bacterial cream on that poke and get you a Band-Aid. Then you can go catch us a fish for dinner." As soon as her ministrations were complete, Jace bolted back to the river.

"Stella, how did everyone stay so calm? How did you know what to do?" McKenzie grimaced. "If it were up to me, I would have rushed him to the emergency room."

Her mother-in-law slid her arm around her waist. "I learned over the years, just like you will—one childhood injury at a time. And with three of my own hooligans— four with Colt—I had to master it all fairly fast. But don't worry, you'll catch on the same way."

McKenzie absently brushed her fingers over her abdomen. "I hope so... someday."

21

Colt rested his hand on Caitlyn's shoulders at the base of her neck. "You ought to call Logan again. He might be able to give us some thoughts on how to locate the fights."

"Good idea." She jabbed the quick dial for her brother's number and tapped the speaker icon. He picked up on the first ring.

"Did you find him?" Logan's voice echoed through the phone, wasting no time on a greeting.

"Not yet. But we breached the property with SWAT and found north of twenty-five dogs chained up here that someone is clearly using for fighting. And it looks like there is space for about twenty more. Most of these pups have torn up ears and scars from attack wounds." Caitlyn's voice dropped. "And there was a shed in back where several dog carcasses were left to rot." Caitlyn swallowed hard and couldn't continue.

Logan's voice softened, but the information he gave

was still difficult to hear. "Many times, these guys test the dogs in fights, and if they don't have an aptitude for brutality, they'll kill them rather than feed them. I've seen dogs shot, drowned, hung, and even electrocuted. The dog fighters claim it's a cultural right, but people who propagate this brutality for sport are pure evil."

Caitlyn shuddered. Colt ground his teeth together. Logan shouldn't have said all of that to his sister—not when Renegade was still missing.

"Listen, Logan," Colt interjected. "The cops found some fliers inside the trailer home that advertise a dog fight happening tonight. The problem is they don't give a location."

"Of course not. They will spread that information by word of mouth for the sake of security. Text me a picture of the flier."

"Hold on." Caitlyn snapped a photo with her phone and sent the text.

"Got it." Logan paused. "Okay. Often, they hold these fighting events within a few miles of where they keep the dogs. These jerks don't want to draw attention to themselves by carting around a bunch of banged up dogs in crates. So, your best bet is going to be asking the local PD to send up a drone to scout the surrounding desert. Fights usually happen late at night or in the early morning hours and can take place in or outside, so you'll be looking for other clues too, like a bunch of cars parked in a random-looking area, especially if there are any trucks loaded with crates nearby."

Colt thanked Logan. "I'll talk to the detective we're working with about coordinating an aerial search." Colt noticed a trail of five or six cars filing up to the busted gate. He tapped Caitlyn's shoulder and pointed at them. "We have to go, Logan. The ASPCA just arrived."

"Okay. Hey, you guys, remember dog fighting is a felony, and the people associated with it are usually into other sorts of dangerous criminal activity. They make hundreds of thousands of dollars on betting on these fights. There's a lot of money at stake and you can expect drugs and firearms, too. Be careful out there. Okay? And call me when you know more."

"Will do." Caitlyn clicked off and hurried after Colt as he jogged over to a white ASPCA truck. Four cars filled with volunteers pulled up behind it.

Colt held his hand out to the driver and introduced himself. "And this is Deputy US Marshal Reed. She's the one who called you."

The volunteers filed out of the cars and studied their surroundings. Their leader shook Caitlyn's hand. "I'm sure glad you did. My name's Mike Zimmer. It's a pleasure to meet you, but boy, I'll tell you, these places never cease to tear me up." He popped open the double doors at the back of the truck. "We have dog handlers with tons of experience helping dogs like these and a team of forensic veterinarians who will do on-site examinations of each animal."

"How will the dogs react to you?" Caitlyn shifted her weight between her feet. "I mean, I imagine this is dangerous work."

"It can be. The dogs are mostly afraid and possibly have never known a kind human. Fear can often lead to aggression, and we're prepared for that, but honestly, most often the dogs are friendly and respond with excitement to new loving people." He rubbed his chin and perched his hands on his hips as he swallowed back emotion. "It truly speaks to the breed. Pit bulls get a bad rap. The ones I've known are sweet puppies. They can go through all this abuse and neglect, and they still just want to love and be loved."

"What happens to them from here?" Caitlyn asked.

"We have a facility we take them to where they'll receive a secondary examination and treatment for any illness or injuries they've received from fighting, abuse, or neglect. The most damaged dogs will stay under veterinary care, but we'll place the others with trained volunteers who can foster the more manageable ones until they're ready for placement. We don't disclose their location because the dogs are a high-dollar asset to the dog fighters. They've been known to break into clinics to steal their dogs back."

Colt watched the dog handlers as they spread out and approached the various animals. One terrified dog tucked his tail and skittered into its ramshackle doghouse, but the others, though tentative, seemed curious and wagged their tails.

"Are any other breeds used in fighting?" A huge part of Colt was hoping someone stole Renegade for breeding instead of this, even though their hunt for Caitlyn's dog was what led them to this awful place.

Zimmer frowned. "It's mostly pits or pit mixes. Sometimes dog fighters will fight their dogs with someone's pet dog for entertainment. They find amusement in watching their trained dogs kill pups who are unprepared. I tell you, these people are sick."

A tear ran, unchecked, down Caitlyn's cheek, and Zimmer drew himself up short. "I'm sorry. Am I talking too much? Sometimes I forget myself."

Colt put his arm around her. "Someone stole Caitlyn's K9 partner a couple of days ago, and we've been trying to find him. The search led us here."

"Oh." Zimmer's face flushed. "I'm very sorry. What kind of dog is he?"

"A Belgian Malinois."

"Hm. I'll keep my ear to the ground. Sometimes I hear things."

Caitlyn pushed away from Colt and squared her shoulders. "Thank you. I'd appreciate that. Colt, we need to talk to Webb about getting a drone in the air while it's still early." She nodded at Zimmer and walked toward the mobile home.

"Thanks, man." Colt shook Zimmer's hand. "The work you do is important."

"Get the word out if you can. Awareness means every-thing, and so do donations."

"You got it." Colt jogged after Caitlyn. She was right. A drone was the next crucial step.

MIKE ZIMMER and his ASPCA team impressed Caitlyn, and she made a mental note to support them financially in the future, but right now her priority remained Renegade.

"Webb!" she shouted to the detective across the yard. "We have an idea." She jogged up to the detectives, who were speaking with the SWAT team leader. "Excuse me, but I just got off the phone with my brother in the FBI. He has some experience with finding and arresting dog fighters. I showed him the flier, and he believes that with that type of notice, the fight is likely close to this breeding and training ground. He suggested we send up a drone to look for possible locations."

The sergeant, clad in black armored gear, glanced down at the badge she had clipped to her belt. "Deputy, I'm Sergeant Don Briggs, PPD SWAT. I think a drone's a great idea. We have two in our tactical vehicle, and we can have them up in five minutes."

"Impressive, Sergeant. Let's get a move on!" Caitlyn glanced over her shoulder to find Colt behind her. "I've got a feeling we're getting close."

"Me too. We're going to find him, Catie. I know it."

"I just hope we're not too late."

By 8:30 p.m., the sky was dark, and the drones had almost completed their grid pattern search of the surrounding fifty square miles, finding nothing but desert and cactus. Caitlyn's earlier optimism waned. The ASPCA team had gathered all the dogs and took them to vet clinics undisclosed to the public in both the Phoenix and Scottsdale areas. And now, Caitlyn paced the dirt yard praying they'd hear from the drone pilots, soon.

A female voice called out from inside the SWAT vehicle. "Sergeant! I might have found something!"

Caitlyn joined Briggs, running to the truck. "What is it?" She leapt into the vehicle and bent over the woman's shoulder. Briggs pushed his way into the cramped space beside her.

The drone pilot pointed at an image on a screen that projected the drone's camera view. "Look, right there. You can barely make it out. But I hovered and noticed that every once in a while, a light goes on and off. It could be a door opening and closing."

"Might be someone's house," Briggs pointed out.

"Yeah, but look at what we see when we go infra-red." She clicked several buttons, and the view changed. Suddenly, they could see cars parked haphazardly around a low, flat building.

Caitlyn searched for the telltale trucks with kennels that Logan told her about. "There! Look." She pointed to the obvious indicators.

Briggs stood tall. "Get me a GPS location on that property," he ordered the drone pilot. Then his voice boomed loud. "Let's roll!"

"Can we ride with you?" Caitlyn asked.

Briggs appeared to dislike the idea, but he acquiesced. "I respect that you're a Deputy Marshal, ma'am, but when we get there, you and the sheriff here must remain behind us. My team will be the ones to breach. Is that understood?"

"Yes. Got it. We'll need a warrant."

"It's already on the way, which is what we should be. Strap in!"

Caitlyn and Colt buckled Kevlar vests around their chests and found empty seats along the bench at the front of the truck and belted themselves in. Within seconds, they were careening through the desert toward what they assumed was a dogfighting pen. Caitlyn checked the clip in her Glock, and Colt did the same.

"Ready?" His hazel eyes pierced hers.

"More than you know."

22

The fishermen left the river without a catch, which McKenzie counted as fortunate since the sun was sinking toward the purple mountain horizon, shimmering like a golden crown above a deep royal-violet cape. Trying to gut a fish and remove trout bones by lantern light was not something she wanted to attempt.

Instead, Stella helped McKenzie and Jace with their Hobo Stew packets. Each person received a large sheet of heavy foil shaped into a bowl. Cubes of beef went in first, and then everyone chose their own add-ons. McKenzie took potatoes, mushrooms, and peppers. She sloshed it with a good amount of soy sauce and wrapped her packet tight. They cooked their supper in the coals of the cheery campfire, while Stella prepared dessert in her cast iron Dutch oven.

"Be careful opening your dinner pouch, Jace. It's hot," Stella admonished. "Dylan, help him, so he doesn't get burned."

McKenzie sat back against a huge log and enjoyed the camp scene while she chewed on her tasty beef and vegetable supper.

Dylan dropped down next to her. "How is it?" Orange firelight danced across his face.

"I had no idea something so simple could taste so delicious." She grinned up at him as he caught a drip of sauce running down her chin with his fingertip.

He licked it off. "Food off a campfire always tastes great. I think it's because you have to earn it, and by the time you eat you're good and hungry."

"You're probably right." She took a bite of a juicy mushroom. "It's been a really great day, hasn't it? Apart from the hook incident, I mean."

"Even with the hook, this has been as close to a perfect day as I've had in a long time."

She glanced at him sideways. "You and your dad seem to be getting along."

"Yeah. It might be for Jace's sake, but I have to admit it's a relief not to be crossing swords with him."

McKenzie breathed in the smokey campfire smell and snuggled up against her husband. "We should probably hit the road right after dessert. It'll be late by the time we get back to the ranch. Jace needs to get to bed, and so do I. I have a doctor's appointment in the morning."

Dylan's beard shifted over his smile. "Are you sure you don't want me to come?"

McKenzie giggled as a loving warmth spread through her. "I'm sure. If you suddenly start attending my appointments when you should be working on the ranch, you'll stir up all sorts of speculation. You can go the next time, if…"

"Okay. I'll plan on taking Jace out to ride the fence with me then. Time the boy learns how to mend barbed wire."

The chocolate-cherry cake Stella served for dessert was surprisingly scrumptious. McKenzie wouldn't have believed Stella could bake cake over a campfire if she hadn't seen it with her own eyes. But the confection held less allure for Jace than old-fashioned marshmallows on a stick. He and John cooked them side by side, competing to see who could toast the perfectly golden puff.

By the time the food and fishing gear were packed away, Jace's eyelids opened and closed like the mouth of a carp. "Hey, kiddo," McKenzie nudged the sleepy boy. "You better ride back to the ranch in the truck with me and Grandma. I think you might fall asleep in the saddle and topple over."

Jace frowned, but Dylan ruffled his hair. "Your aunt is right. Can't have you dropping off your horse. You can lie down in the back seat, and I'll pony Whiskey behind us."

Jace's effort to complain lacked energy and conviction, and soon he was resting in the backseat of the old pickup. McKenzie and Stella bounced along the rough mountain road back to Reed Ranch. She looked over her shoulder to see Jace curled up on the Navajo blanket spread across the bench seat, sound asleep.

"He's a cute kid, don't you think?" she asked Stella.

"Sure is. He's the spitting image of Colt at the same age."

"That's what Caitlyn says, too." McKenzie's fingers

flitted over her belly. She prayed she was pregnant, but she'd been late before. She'd taken the home tests and had been disappointed. Again, the home test showed two solid pink lines, so with cautious hope she'd made an appointment with an OBGYN in Spearfish. It wasn't that she thought Blake wasn't a good doctor, but she didn't want any rumors flying around. If she went to his office, someone would whisper and the whole town would know the results practically before she did.

Stella's mouth, lit by the lights of the dashboard, curled gently. "You seem happy."

McKenzie smiled and adjusted her seat on the bouncing cushion.

"And I'm happy for you." Stella kept her gaze on the dirt road.

"What for?"

"For what you'll tell me when you're ready."

McKenzie's face heated, and she touched her hot cheeks with cool fingers. "What do you mean?" she asked but didn't need to.

"Not a thing. But I will admit, I always wondered if Dylan's sons would look just like him, too."

"How do you do that?" McKenzie was both startled and impressed.

"Do what, dear?" Stella's eyes sparkled.

"Know everything."

She responded with a soft laugh. "Being a mother teaches you many things."

"Like how to remove fishhooks?"

"Yes, and how to pay attention to all the little things.

How to read the undercurrent. Don't worry, I won't say a word to anyone."

McKenzie shook her head and remained in quiet thought the rest of the way home. When they got there, she woke Jace and helped him from the truck. She walked behind him, holding him steady, as he trundled through the house and fell into bed. After tucking him in, she and Stella unpacked the truck and had everything tidied away by the time Dylan and John rode into the barnyard.

The men brushed down the horses and put them up for the night before Dylan and McKenzie went inside to check on Jace. He wasn't in his bed. She checked the bathroom. The boy wasn't there either.

"Jace?" Dylan's voice boomed through the house. Each spot they searched, they found empty. McKenzie's pulse bumped up along with her pace. Soon, she was running from room to room. They looked everywhere—all the places a boy might get to, but still no Jace.

McKenzie grabbed a flashlight and flew outside with Dylan on her heels, yelling Jace's name into the night. John and Stella joined them in the barnyard, each carrying their own light. John went inside the barn. Stella ran out toward the arena and the tree swing beyond.

Panic caused McKenzie to freeze in her tracks until Dylan pointed to the kennels. "McKenzie, you check the runs. I'll look inside the office." Dylan threw open the door and turned on all the lights. She searched the corners of each dog kennel with her bright light. Soon all the dogs were awake, making loud barking and howling complaints.

In the last pen on the right, her beam tripped on a boy's untied Converse tennis shoe. McKenzie followed the foot inside it with her light, tracking up the leg and across Jace's sleeping form, which was curled against the gray body of Storm. The dog stared at her with his blue eyes, but he didn't move a muscle other than his stub of a tail that twitched back and forth.

When the light flooded his face, Jace blinked open his eyes. "What's going on?" he asked as he rubbed them.

"Jace! Thank God!" McKenzie turned toward the offices and yelled, "Dylan! I found him!" She crouched outside the kennel. "What are you doing in there?"

"I came out to say goodnight to Storm, and he was crying. So, I went in his kennel to pet him a little—to make him feel better. But I guess I fell asleep."

McKenzie's heart squeezed. The natural relationship developing between Jace, and this supposedly fierce pit bull moved her deeply.

Dylan ran to her side and glowered at the boy. "You scared us, young man. We didn't know where you were."

"I'm sorry, I just wanted to tell Storm he was safe."

McKenzie placed her hand on Dylan's arm. "I found him in there, sound asleep, wrapped around his new best friend."

Dylan frowned. "Didn't we already talk to you about going into the kennels without asking?"

Jace's earnest boyish face looked up at them. "Yes, but he was crying, Uncle Dylan. You told me it was our job to take care of our animals, and that they come first on a ranch. So, I went into Storm's kennel to remind him I love him."

Dylan chuffed and then grinned. "Well, I can't argue with that, but listen to me, Jace. You must always tell us where you're going. This is a big place, and there are lots of dangerous things around here. We have to know where you are at all times."

"That's right, sweetheart, and besides," with a full heart, McKenzie bumped Dylan's arm with her shoulder, "Uncle Dylan wouldn't have told you no... in fact, he probably would have crawled right in there with you."

23

Colt gripped the leather loop attached to the roof to steady himself as the SWAT vehicle screeched around a corner on the way to what looked like a dogfighting venue that had been located with the drone. He watched their progress through the windshield. It seemed as though they were catapulting down one long, winding desert road to nowhere. And the visibility got worse as the sky grew darker.

A dim green light illuminated what little Colt could see inside the SWAT transport. High-powered rifles and other tools such as a steel door ram, and an intense-looking Halligan bar used for prying locked entries open, hung clipped in place to the walls above them. The team of seven sat on the side benches and were laser focused on their leader who detailed their approach strategy.

Briggs addressed his unit, "Alright, listen up. This may look like a bunch of punks and amateurs but take nothing for granted. Intel suggests there is far more than dogfighting going on. Expect dealers with drugs and guns who won't go down without a fight.

"We will breach with the assumption that the dogfighters are heavily armed. Remain vigilant and watch each other's back. Reed, Branson, you two are with me. Stay on my six. Got it?"

Colt gave Briggs a nod and glanced across the truck to Caitlyn, who gave riveted attention to the team leader's instructions. A surge of pride filled Colt's chest. He was both impressed and terrified by her determination and resilience.

"Got it," she replied, her dark eyes intense with purpose.

The vehicle slowed, and all lights extinguished. The driver was a guy they called Doogie, after the teenaged doctor on the TV show *Doogie Howser, M.D.*, because he looked like he was about fifteen.

Briggs listened as the driver reported what he saw. "Lots of cars and trucks parked randomly around the structure. Could be bogies in or near any of them. There's a minimum of two armed guards at each visible entrance. With the noise coming from the building, we can assume the event is in progress. The distraction will give us an advantage."

A sudden movement on the side of an old Chevy 4x4 caught Colt's eye. He squinted for clearer focus. Two men standing in between the truck and a Jeep exchanged items he couldn't quite make out, but Colt recognized their movements: each man passing something to the other while suspiciously glancing over their shoulders. "Looks like a drug deal going down. Eleven o'clock."

Doogie, who kept the black SWAT vehicle in the shadows, ceased forward progress. Briggs peered out the window and then whispered his next orders. "Alright team, fill the gaps and stay liquid. Silvers and Pine—exit and investigate. Neutralize the threat."

The scouts nodded, gripped their glass-bedded, scoped, bolt-action rifles with their free-floating barrels and opened the back doors. Briggs murmured, "Here we go!" The two men silently dropped out of the vehicle.

Adrenaline bubbled through Colt's veins. As a small-town sheriff, he'd never been a part of this type of covert operation, and apart from his concern over Caitlyn and Renegade, he was almost giddy to be included in such a mission.

He glanced at his wife, who stared intensely at Briggs, awaiting her orders. Caitlyn's body vibrated with high-voltage energy. Her eyes gleamed with purpose—the only one she had in that moment. Renegade.

Now that the back doors of the SWAT vehicle were open, the op went silent, and their leader directed the team using hand signals. Colt and Caitlyn unholstered their weapons and waited for Briggs to exit ahead of them. Carrying borrowed ballistic shields for cover, they stayed tight on his back, following Briggs' every move.

Once they were outside, fierce barking, growling, and pain-drenched yelping filled the night air. Laughter, and whoops of victory clashed with groan of defeat. Caitlyn pressed the side of Colt's forearm. He turned to her and saw frigid fear etched in tight lines around her mouth and eyes.

Remaining silent, Colt covered her hand with his and

nodded, hoping she interpreted his gesture as encourage-
ment. Her terror was not for herself, or even for him.
She'd been in far more dangerous situations than this. It
was for what Renegade was probably facing. If not here
tonight, then somewhere else. He hated thinking of Ren
forced into a pen where his choice was to fight or die. But
if that was the case, Colt's confidence rested in Renegade.

Briggs motioned for them and one other of his team
members to follow him. He whispered orders to the
entire unit through a microphone in his helmet, but since
Colt and Caitlyn didn't have the high-tech gear, he
continued using hand signals for them.

Together, they gripped their weapons and shields as
they lined up and crept to the back door of the dilapi-
dated building. The voices inside screaming with
emotion gave them cover. Some cheered and others
cursed while barking, growling, and pain-filled yelps told
the story of two innocent dogs fighting for their lives
inside a pen.

A mixed lump of nausea and anger formed in Colt's
throat. He wished he could protect Caitlyn from seeing
all of this somehow. Briggs motioned for them to stand at
the sides of the entrance. They were preparing to
announce their presence before the breach when Colt
noted a man, approximately six-foot-four and two-
hundred and fifty-pounds, stride by a crack in the door
frame. Not only was the guy huge, but he carried an
assault rifle. Colt waved at Briggs and motioned for him
to stop.

Briggs peered through the opening, nodded, and
directed his backup with hand signals. The SWAT officer

approached the split and slid a flexible scope with a camera attached to the end through the hole. They watched the video projection on a small screen strapped to his forearm.

Briggs addressed the team on his mic. "There's a lot of firepower inside, which signifies a lot more is going on in there than dog fighting. Pine, find a vantage point and be ready with your long rifle. We'll flush these dirtbags out of here."

"Doogie, announce our arrival over the truck's megaphone. Anyone who remains inside is protecting something. My guess is drugs. Let the runners go. PPD uniforms have the perimeter surrounded. These scumbags won't get far. At my ready, we'll breach on my command. Clear?"

24

———

Caitlyn was glad she'd brought three extra clips for her Glock, but her weapon was no match for the fully automatic assault rifles the guards inside carried. Still, on the chance that Renegade was in there, she'd do and risk whatever it took to get to him.

In a barely audible voice, Briggs said, "We go on three." He held up his fingers. "One... two...three." As he said three, he pointed toward the door.

Because she and Colt weren't outfitted like the rest of the SWAT team, when the officer bashed open the door with the steel ram, they entered behind him and the Sergeant. The other teams entered at the same moment, causing chaos and panic among the dirt bags who were in attendance. Men forced their way out the doors, even jumping through windows to avoid getting arrested.

The four law enforcement officers in Caitlyn's group all carried their firearms at the ready. All were careful to use the rolling heel-toe step that prevented tripping as they filed in through the entrance, alternating directions, with Caitlyn bringing up the rear.

Briggs held his hand up to bring them to a halt. While they stood still, he silently approached the back of the huge guard who was striding toward the ruckus beyond. Briggs pressed his pistol against his head and ordered him to freeze and release his weapon.

Without stopping, Goliath bent forward and pivoted, swinging his rifle around toward the SWAT commander. Briggs hammer-chopped the guy's arms and rammed his elbow up into his larynx. The giant man tried to cry out with his pain but could only cough as he fell backward. Cheering from the crowd farther down the hall absorbed the man's choking gurgle.

In a smooth movement, Briggs gripped the rifle barrel and used it as leverage against the big man. He then wrenched the weapon away from him, but not before the guy squeezed off twenty or thirty rounds that peppered the wall and ceiling. Throwing the guard onto the floor, Briggs pressed his knee into the man's broad back. The commander yanked the man's hands together, cinching his wrists into metal cuffs.

From there, the event sped up. Men yelled, guns fired, and dogs barked in terror. People scattered everywhere like cockroaches when the light turns on in a New York City kitchen. Those few that remained had business they wanted to protect and proved it with firepower.

Caitlyn heard a pack of dogs barking frantically. She left the drug and gun mayhem to Colt and the SWAT team. Choosing not to remain with them, she dashed toward a closed door down the hall at their rear. The barking intensified and she reached for the handle. It was unlocked.

She shoved the door open but remained behind the wall for cover. Dogs barked and howled, but when no shots were fired, she peered around the dark storage room. The stench of dog crap was unmistakable, and she gagged and coughed. Carrying a small flashlight in her left hand, she held it under the grip of her gun, bracing her firing hand as she searched the room. Crates containing dogs of different sizes packed the space from wall to wall. Some animals lunged and snapped at her as she passed by, while others cowered. All of them had bleeding wounds to show for their efforts in the fighting pen.

"Renegade? Ren, are you in here?" Caitlyn tried to whisper, but desperation added agency to her voice. "Renegade? Please be here."

With her flashlight, she studied the face of each imprisoned hound, but none of them were her beloved Ren. Caitlyn moved quickly to the door and slipped back into the hallway, closing the injured dogs in the room behind her. When this was all over, she'd bring help.

The shouting in the building decreased as more spectators ran from the scene, but the staccato of gunfire continued. Caitlyn inched farther down the corridor. Behind her, she heard the calls of SWAT members as they cleared rooms along their way.

The building on her side was eerily quiet other than the echoes of frightened dogs. She shouldn't have peeled off on her own, and she'd pay hell for it later, but the thing was, the cops were more interested in arresting felons than finding her dog. She had only one objective. Renegade. Focusing on her single goal, Caitlyn moved deeper into the structure.

Another door, similar to the one she'd come from, stood at the end of the hall and she ran toward it. Her heart beat so hard her lungs had to fight for room to breathe. Before she turned the knob, she sucked in deep breaths to slow her pulse. As soon as it steadied, she reached for the handle. It was locked.

She tried it again, and the rattling stirred up the dogs on the other side of the door. Desperation overcame her senses, she set down her shield and backed away about fifteen feet. The only way into the room was through the locked door, so she tucked her shoulder and ran full force, busting through the flimsy wood. It flew open, sending splinters sailing through the air as she stumbled into the room.

Her body immediately responded to the jolt. Her knees buckled and a blinding light shot through her brain. Her ears rang and her stomach heaved. Somewhere in her head, an internal voice screamed at her to take cover. She scooted across the cement floor until her back pressed against the wall, but she couldn't stop now. Once she found Renegade, she would have time to rest.

Ruff! Rrrrrufff! The single sound she'd been searching for, the one she would recognize anywhere—even through the mass of barking dogs. Weak though it was, Renegade's bark rang out from somewhere near the back.

"Renegade! Ren! I'm here, boy! I'm coming." Dizzy and still disoriented, her thigh slammed into a crate, and a set of vicious fangs gnashed at her. She jumped away and pushed on, shoving cages to the side as fast as she could—dodging around various sizes of kennels. "Ren, where are you?" she cried.

Snap. Click. The unmistakable sound of a bullet entering the chamber of a pistol sounded right behind her left ear. All the hair on Caitlyn's body pricked up, and she froze, mid-lunge.

25

"Well, well, well. What do we have here? You're not wearing a uniform, but you sure as hell smell like a cop." The man belonging to the gun sniffed her hair. "A sweet-smelling lady cop, that is."

"I'm a deputy US marshal." She kept her voice calm and confident though she cursed herself for letting this guy get the jump on her. "I'm sure you know you're already surrounded, so do the smart thing and give yourself up."

"Why would I do that when I've got me a marshal to trade for my freedom? Now real slow like, hand me your gun. And don't try to pull anything or I'll blast your spine in two." He jabbed the end of his gun into her back to make his point.

"Okay, okay. Stay calm." If Caitlyn was the only one in the room, she could spin and press the muzzle of his pistol off to the side, taking the weapon from him with her momentum, but there were too many dogs in the room, and if he fired, the wild shot could hit one of them. It could hit Ren.

Renegade's barking was no longer weak. He was loud and forceful, ramming himself against the door of his cage and clawing at the lock. As relieved as she was that she'd found him, she was equally terrified he was still very much in danger. Caitlyn wanted to reassure him but didn't dare do anything to upset the man who was pressing a gun to her spine or to draw specific attention to her dog.

"I'm perfectly calm." The man behind her nudged her with his weapon. "Hold your gun up with two fingers."

Caitlyn did as he asked, and he snatched the Glock out of her hand, tossing it approximately ten feet to the right. She noted the location with both her peripheral vision and by the sound it made hitting the cement floor. He reached around her body with his free hand, yanked her back against his chest. Unclipping her protective vest, he reached his hand inside to grope her breast. Bile-fueled fury scorched her throat as he man-handled her.

But then he made a crucial error.

His gun slid from her back to her side as he reached around her for a better feel, which subsequently gave her room to maneuver. In a flash, Caitlyn smacked his gun arm with her left hand, pressing the weapon away from her body, effectively redirecting the shot. She hooked his wrist in the crook of her elbow, controlling the direction the weapon pointed. He panicked and stepped backward, giving her the advantage. She spun, and drove her right elbow into his face, breaking his nose.

As he reeled from the pain, she wrapped her fingers

around the barrel of the gun and bent his hand backwards. Twisting, she forced the weapon from his grip. With all her strength, she swung the gun, hammering the butt into the side of his head twice before he fell to his knees.

Caitlyn sprang back to give herself more space. She reached to the floor for her Glock, and as soon as she had her gun in hand, she released the clip of her captive's weapon and let it clatter to the ground. Everything in her screamed to run to Renegade, but she had to call for backup first.

"Colt!" she yelled out to the doorway. The shout was like shattered glass exploding inside her skull. She breathed through the pain and stared at her captive. In the dim light from the hall, she recognized the man kneeling on the floor before her. He was the same man who had rudely bumped into her in the parking lot on the first day of the Police K9 Trials. The man suspected of ramming into their car two nights ago. "Melville Rankin. We've been looking for you. You are under arrest for vehicular manslaughter." Her voice caught and she took another breath. "For leaving the scene of an accident, and for whatever other charges will come against you for your involvement in dog theft and fighting. That's a minimum of two felonies."

Caitlyn held her gun aimed steadily on Rankin, but stupid in his anger and humiliation, he yanked a knife from a belt scabbard.

"Put the knife down, Rankin. Don't be a fool. I will drop you way before you can get to me." In truth, she knew he could throw the knife faster than she could respond to his movement. If his aim was true, she could be dead before she had the chance to shoot.

Rankin sprang toward her from his position on the floor.

Without hesitation, Caitlyn fired twice—a double tap to his head and heart.

Her yell for help and the gun shots brought the backup she needed. As soon as Colt and Briggs arrived, Caitlyn ran to the cage imprisoning Renegade. She pulled on the door, but it was sealed with a heavy-duty padlock and wouldn't budge.

"Oh Ren! I found you! You're alive!" His high-pitched barks greeted her. Renegade pawed anxiously at the bars of his pen and licked at her fingers through the slats. "It's okay, buddy. I'll get you out of here." She turned and called over her shoulder. "I need some bolt cutters over here, right now!"

The overhead lights snapped on, and Colt skidded to his knees beside her. He threw his arms around her and held her tight against him. "Thank God, you're okay, Catie. When I heard the gunshots behind us…"

"I'm fine, Colt. I'm okay. And we found him! We found Renegade!"

Colt's eyes narrowed as he looked at her. "Why is your Kevlar vest unclipped?"

Caitlyn bit her lip. The truthful answer would push Colt over the edge, but she couldn't keep it from him. "The man who attacked me unbuckled it. Which worked in my favor because he was close enough for me to take his weapon away from him."

"Why would he unbuckle your vest?"

She sunk her teeth into her lip again, this time drawing blood from her overworked skin. "He, uh... he felt me up. But like I said, the distraction is how I got his gun. Then when he came at me with the knife, I had to shoot him." A deadly hazel heat flashed in Colt's eyes, so she changed the subject. "None of that matters right now. We need to get Renegade out of this cage immediately! Look at him. He's bleeding from a cut under his eye and his ear is torn."

Her voice caught on emotion, and she reached her fingers through the narrow rungs. "And look at his fore-leg! He has an awful-looking bite wound. I think it might be infected. What have you gone through, my poor guy? Oh, Ren! I'm so sorry." Renegade whined, desperately licking her fingertips.

A young SWAT officer ran into the room with the requested bolt cutters and Briggs pointed to Caitlyn. Colt took the hefty tool from the cop, and Caitlyn backed away from the latch to give him room. The powerful vice sliced through the thick metal with ease, and the lock fell into pieces on the ground.

Renegade sprang through the open door and lunged into Caitlyn's arms, knocking her back onto her butt. She held him so tight, he probably couldn't breathe, but it didn't stop his tongue from slathering every bare inch of her face and neck.

She laughed while tears ran down her cheeks at the same time. All the stress and strain of the past couple of days coursed out of her body all at once. The dogs in the other crates howled with excitement.

Colt stroked Renegade. "You had to know she'd find

you one way or another, boy. You two are the tightest team I've ever known." He received a juicy slurp of love as he patted Renegade's shoulder and stood. Over the din in the room, Colt's deep voice demanded a veterinarian. "All these dogs need emergency care. Someone call the ASPCA."

Briggs looked pale in the florescent lighting. Caitlyn cocked her head. "What's wrong?"

"This man…"

"Rankin? What about him?"

"Yeah." Briggs crossed his arms over his chest. "I've seen him before."

Caitlyn held her breath, and Colt went to look at the body. "Where?"

"He was at a bar with a Phoenix K9 cop. Officer Berkley. They're stepbrothers." He ran his hand over his face. "Shit."

Pieces tumbled together in Caitlyn's wounded mind like an ornate set of metal clock gears, their teeth lining up and realigning. "Berkley is the cop who leant us the K9 vehicle when we came into town for the dog trials."

"Yeah." Colt's brows furrowed. "He's a good dude. But you're saying Berkley and Rankin are related? What the hell?"

Caitlyn held Renegade in her lap. "Didn't he say his dog was missing, too? Could they have been in this together?"

Colt planted his hands firmly on his hips. "Are you saying you think he sold his K9 partner to these monsters?"

"I don't know." Caitlyn stroked her dog as she thought

about it. "But one thing I do know is dogs like his and Renegade are worth a ton of money."

"My thoughts exactly." Briggs quietly conferred with his second in command, who bobbed his chin and ran to accomplish his orders. "We'll get to the bottom of this, but at this point, we cannot allow anyone else to enter this crime scene. Not even veterinarians. We won't have this place secured for hours. ATF is here, and they're still searching for more drugs and weapons. Reed, you'll need to give your statement to the detectives."

"We can't wait for that." Colt stepped toward Briggs, emphasizing his urgency. "K9 Renegade is a fellow law enforcement officer, and he needs immediate medical attention. Caitlyn can come to the department later and give her statement."

Having heard their discussion from the outer room, Detective Webb leaned his head into the airless space. "That's not a problem. I'll take you in my car. Whenever you're ready to go. It's still early, but we can take him to an all-night emergency vet, if you want."

Caitlyn was weak with gratitude. "Thank you, Darin." She glanced at her watch. It was half-past six in the morning. None of them had slept in over twenty-four hours, and she and Colt had only a few hours of sleep before that. A huge yawn forced her jaws open.

Webb smiled at her use of his first name. "It's the least we can do for him—and you."

As soon as she saw Renegade limping when he tried to walk, she lifted him and headed toward the door and the detective waiting outside.

"Caitlyn," Colt's tone had hardened. The fact that he

used her full name, which he never did, stopped her in her stride. She turned to face him and raised her brows in question. He lifted Renegade from her arms. "I'm glad you found Renegade, and that he's going to be okay, but I am really pissed that you took off by yourself. You could have been killed. It was a stupid move. One that with your experience, I'm surprised you made. And, by the way, you're not supposed to carry anything." He carried her dog and placed him inside Webb's car. "Go take Ren to the vet. But this discussion isn't over."

Her teeth clamped together. She lifted her chin and narrowed her eyes. Anger percolated through her blood. How dare he talk to her like that in front of their peers? "I don't answer to you, Colt Branson."

"Yes. You do." With that, he walked back to the building and helped the uniformed cops string up the crime scene tape.

26

———

A deep orange orb brightened the eastern horizon as McKenzie drove toward Spearfish. Her doctor's appointment was first thing that morning, and she didn't want to be late. Today she'd find out if what she hoped and prayed for was a reality. She'd know for sure whether or not she was pregnant.

There was no real reason not to believe the home tests. Everyone said they were extremely reliable. Still, she wanted official confirmation from a doctor and then a full list of what to eat, how to exercise—everything. Silken wings fluttered in her belly, and she imagined it was a baby's fingers. Though, of course, if she was pregnant, she knew from the pile of fertility and pregnancy books on her nightstand, that she wasn't far enough along to feel anything. Dylan teased her about all the books she read, telling her that reading wasn't what was going to get her pregnant.

It was over an hour's drive to the doctor's office in the South Dakota town, which was why she chose it. She wanted to keep her business to herself, and in the tiny mountain burg of Moose Creek, someone at the medical clinic would leak her news and it would be all over town by lunchtime. This way, she and Dylan could hold their secret just between them for a little while. Well, sort of. Stella already suspected.

If and when McKenzie and Dylan got pregnant, and when they were ready to announce it, she would submit herself to Blake Kennedy's capable care. But until then, she preferred to remain anonymous.

McKenzie smiled, remembering how Dylan had tried to act nonchalant about her appointment this morning, but he couldn't hide the hope in his eyes. He wasn't any good at subterfuge. None of the Reeds were, hence, the family trait of brutal honesty and directness. A Reed-ism she'd had to get used to.

Surprisingly, the OBGYN waiting room was already packed full when she entered. Apparently, these doctors started their day early. McKenzie signed in and waited in a seat next to an enormous saltwater tank filled with brightly colored tropical fish and a miniature sunken pirate ship. Exuberant toddlers ran past her in and out of the toy corner, and McKenzie closed her eyes, listening to their chatter. What would it be like to have a child's laughter fill the rooms in the ranch house?

Thirty-five minutes after her scheduled appointment, the receptionist called her name, and she followed the woman back to an exam room. "You're here for a pregnancy check. Is that correct?"

"Yes." Her nerves crackled with anxiety.

"And you've had a positive home test?"

"Yes," McKenzie repeated.

"Okay. Let me get your vitals, and I'll take some blood. Then the doctor will be in to see you."

The nurse was remarkably efficient and left McKenzie sitting at the foot of the exam table to await the results. Ten minutes later, she wished she would have brought a magazine from the lobby with her. With no reading material, she opted for a mindless scroll through Instagram. She followed tons of dog-oriented accounts and loved to see canine portraits, puppies, and watch the myriad training videos.

Finally, a light tap sounded on the door and a woman in her late fifties peeked in. She had a round, kind face framed by graying brown curls and wore a white lab coat over maroon polyester pants and a floral blouse. "Hello, Ms. Reed?"

"Yes." McKenzie tucked her phone into her purse.

"Good morning. Sorry for the wait. I'm Doctor Tidwell." She reached to shake McKenzie's hand. "It's been a busy morning around here already, and we're just getting started."

The doctor sat on an adjustable stool and brought McKenzie's medical chart up on the computer. She scanned through McKenzie's history and her recent answers to their check-in questionnaire before she swiveled to face her with a kind smile. "Well, good news. You are indeed pregnant."

McKenzie was glad she was sitting because she instantly became dizzy. Pure effervescent joy bubbled through her blood. She must have swayed because the doctor sprang to her feet and held onto McKenzie's shoulder until she stabilized.

"Easy there. Did you have breakfast?"

McKenzie shook her head. "Not yet. I was going to get something on my way home."

"Well, that's lesson number one. You must eat all the calories and nutrition necessary for your little one to grow healthy and strong. Breakfast, first thing in the morning, is non-negotiable. If you get morning sickness, you might need to wait until you can hold the food down, but then a protein-heavy meal is still imperative."

"Okay." A huge smile forced its way across her face. Even though McKenzie had taken the home test, the medical confirmation still overwhelmed her, and she gazed at the doctor. "I'm really going to have a baby?"

"You really are." The doctor squeezed her shoulder before returning to her seat. She went over everything McKenzie needed and what she should expect in her first trimester.

"How far along do you think I am?"

They discussed dates and typed them into the computer. "You are at almost eight weeks now, which gives you an approximate due date of May 21st. That's a lovely time of year to have a little one."

"May 21st," McKenzie murmured in wonder.

When she left the office, McKenzie practically floated on clouds on the way out to the truck. She wanted to call Dylan right away, but then decided it might be more fun to tell him in person. Would they announce it to John and Stella at dinner that night, or would they keep the news a secret between them for a little while?

An icy chill of apprehension skittered down her back. What about Caitlyn? How could she ever tell her best friend that she was having a baby when Caitlyn had so recently lost hers? Would McKenzie's pregnancy break Caitlyn's heart? She didn't know, but it was out of her control. Eventually, her bump would be obvious whether she told her dear friend or not. Still, a small cushion of time might help.

McKenzie sat in the cab, thinking about what to do next. Dylan was out mending fences with Jace that morning, so even if she relented and called him now, his phone never had coverage out there. She was forced to stick to her original plan of watching his expression when she gave him the news. After which, they could decide together about when to tell everyone else.

She pulled out onto the street, and her phone rang over the car speakers. It was Caitlyn. *Crap*! Maybe she shouldn't answer.

Guilt swirled at the base of her belly. She couldn't ignore Caitlyn's call, so she answered tentatively. "Hello? Caitlyn? How are you?"

"Hey, Kenze. I'm good. I'm great, in fact. We found him! I have Ren with me right now!"

"Oh!" Relief poured from McKenzie's head down to her toes. "Thank God! Where was he? Is he okay?"

She listened as Caitlyn recounted their search, and how she'd found him. "I'm at the emergency vet now. She's already patched up the more superficial wounds, but Ren has an infected dog bite on his foreleg. The vet here wants to do surgery to clean out the wound and possibly repair any ligament or tendon damage. I don't know what to do."

"I'm so happy you found him and that he's okay. I'm thrilled. As far as his care, I can't answer if he should have surgery or not. Is there any way you could have that veterinarian send his findings up here to Doc Moore so you could get a second opinion?"

"That's a good idea. Where are you? You sound like you're driving."

McKenzie dreaded talking about herself right then because she didn't want to slip up. She desperately wanted to share her wonderful news with her best friend. Especially now that she reunited with Renegade. But she was afraid that her news would come as a crushing blow on the heels of Caitlyn's miscarriage. So, she stuck to her previous decision.

"I am. Just out running errands." McKenzie strove for a light and carefree tone, but it backfired. She should have known better.

"What kind of errands?" Caitlyn's voice sounded speculative.

"Oh, this and that."

There was a long pause, but Caitlyn must have decided not to pursue her curiosity. "How's Jace? I know Colt wishes he was there with him."

"We're enjoying him. He's... well, he's such a boy!" The women laughed together.

"That, he is. I hope he's behaving himself."

"He is, and your brother is loving having a mini-ranch hand around."

"Good. Well, depending on what the veterinarians

determine, we should be home tomorrow or the next day. I suppose if Ren needs surgery, it might take longer. If that's the case, I'll tell Colt to fly home to relieve you from babysitting."

"It's not really babysitting when it's family. I know John and Stella love having Jace, too. In fact, he might come back to you guys a little spoiled."

"No surprise there. We really appreciate you and Dylan taking such good care of him. Listen, the vet just came out. I'll call you later when I know more." Caitlyn signed off, leaving McKenzie flushed with relief that she hadn't given her secret away. There would be plenty of time to tell Caitlyn and Colt about the newest Reed family member. She splayed her hand across her abdomen as a wave of pure elation filled her heart.

27

The desert heat stretched its fiery fingers into every vacant space, and the temperature in Phoenix crawled steadily up the thermometer. Caitlyn was with Renegade at the emergency vet, but Colt had stayed with Detective Albrecht at the crime scene. Together they would go the department headquarters and see if they could find Dan Berkley.

No cop ever wanted the task of telling another police family that a relative was dead, but this time the men carried the added weight of not knowing if the K9 cop was complicit in the dognapping and dogfighting incidents.

Detective Webb had helped Caitlyn carry Renegade into the lobby of the veterinary clinic where they were met by two vet techs whose tennis shoes squeaked on the brilliant white floor tile. Before they even allowed Caitlyn to explain Renegade's injuries, she had to fill out forms and fork over her credit card for a three-hundred-dollar deposit. Caitlyn idly wondered if she'd be reimbursed for the expense, but figured she wouldn't since Renegade had not been on official duty when he was abducted. On the other hand, their search for him revealed a huge dogfighting operation with ties to drug and gun smuggling. She should not only be reimbursed, but Ren should get an award.

Once her card information went through, she and Renegade were shown to an exam room. The techs lifted Ren onto the stainless-steel table. The taller of the two asked, "Will he stay up here, or do you think he'd be better off on the floor until the vet can see you?"

"He'll stay." Caitlyn gave Ren an open hand sign and he rested his nose between his paws.

"The vet will be in soon." With that, the techs left.

Webb took a seat, but Caitlyn remained standing next to her dog. "His leg wound is oozing. The bite doesn't look fresh. He must have had to fight before last night."

"Hard to say. I'm just glad you found him alive. The wounds will heal."

"You're right. I don't need to agonize over what I don't know, but the whole thing breaks my heart. I hated leaving all those other dogs back there. They need medical care, too."

"They'll get it. Don't worry. As soon as they can, the investigative team will let ASPCA in and those dogs will be rescued. Think of all the animals you've helped save yesterday and today. That ought to put a smile on your face."

The vet came in and after an initial exam, asked Caitlyn and Webb to wait in the lobby while they took Renegade back for x-rays.

"He's a federal K9, and he's just been through a very traumatic experience. I'm not sure he'll go with you willingly if I'm not there."

"I understand. We'll give him a little something to ease his nerves right now, while you're by his side. But then, we'll need to take him back on his own."

Caitlyn didn't want to be separated from her dog for even half a minute, but she understood they had to keep the facility as sanitary as possible. So, after the doctor dosed Ren with some happy juice, she and Webb went out to the reception area to wait.

It seemed an eternity before the vet came out to get her. "Deputy Reed, if you'll follow me to my office, I can show you the x-rays and discuss Renegade's care plan."

She let out a pent-up breath and followed the doctor while Webb stayed behind. "Is his leg fractured?" she asked.

"No, but there likely is extensive tendon and ligament damage. And there are several areas that should be cleaned for better healing, while Renegade is under anesthesia." She pointed at the spots of concern on the image with her pen. "Your dog has many scrapes and contusions. We've cleaned those up and rest will be the best medicine to heal them, but I'm concerned about this leg. I'd like to get him into surgery right away."

Caitlyn would do anything for Ren, and that included *not* forcing him into vet care he didn't need. Call her a skeptic, but she wanted to discuss her options with someone she trusted and who wasn't as emotional as she was right then. "I need to think about it and talk with our personal vet. Can you give me some time?"

"Yes, but it would be easier on your sweet dog if he didn't have to wake up from one sedative only to be given another. It's just something to consider. We don't want him to suffer unnecessarily."

Her gut tightened, and she always trusted her gut. "Let me make a phone call. I'll let you know as soon as I can."

Caitlyn returned to the waiting room. "Hey, Darin. You don't have to wait here with me. I could be awhile. The vet wants to do surgery on that leg."

"Okay. If you're sure. I'm too old for these all-nighters anymore. I'll get your husband back to your rental car so he can pick you up here."

"That's okay. I can call an Uber when I'm ready to leave. You've been terrific." She hugged the tall detective and pecked his cheek. "I hope to see you before we fly home, but if not, thanks for everything."

As soon as Webb exited, Caitlyn slumped in her chair, relieved she didn't have to keep up the appearance of being on top of everything. She was too tired to keep up her brave front. Closing her eyes, the image of shooting Rankin played in vivid color through her mind.

Why did he have to come at her with that knife? Damn him. She did her best to stay angry at the man, but deep inside it sickened her to take his life. And the worst of it was she knew it would never have happened if she would have stayed with Colt and the SWAT unit. She had been impatient and impulsive. Her head throbbed with the acknowledgement of her bad decision.

Colt had been right, though it still angered her that he felt as though he could order her around and chastise her in front of the other cops. She'd eventually have to wade through all of this in therapy, but for now she wanted to change the subject.

While she was waiting, she had called McKenzie. Her phone rang several times before her friend's tentative voice answered the call. Caitlyn had told her how they had come to find Ren and that he was currently at the emergency vet and that she wanted to do surgery on his leg.

McKenzie suggested she call Doc Moore, and Caitlyn wondered why she hadn't already done that. Her brain didn't seem to be working on all cylinders. But when she asked what her sister-in-law was up to, McKenzie sounded suspiciously vague.

Something was up, but she hadn't had the energy to pursue it. So, she asked about Jace. Poor kid, being dropped off and then abandoned by her and Colt. Guilt prodded her already exhausted conscience. All she wanted right now was to be home sitting by the fire with Renegade, Colt, and Jace.

She dialed Doctor Moore and relayed all the details she knew. "With all that information, would you recommend surgery?"

Doctor Moore was silent for a long moment before he cleared his throat. "Why don't you ask the veterinarian there to send me all the lab work and imaging? I'm not sure I would rush into surgery, but I do recommend flushing the wound while he's still asleep and getting him on antibiotics right away. I will call you with my opinion once I see all the information."

"Thanks, Doc."

"You're welcome. I can only imagine how relieved you are that you found him. And with what you've gone through, I'm sure the happy news is helping you feel better."

Helping her feel better? Oh—of course—somehow the news of her accident and the loss of their baby had already made the rounds in Moose Creek. Her family wouldn't have said anything, but Wes Cooper, Colt's deputy, probably let two innocent words slip, and that's all it took. Damn. But... "What happy news?"

"About the puppies. Athena and Renegade were successful. Surely McKenzie told you about that? You'll have little Renegades running all around soon."

What? Why hadn't McKenzie said anything to her? That must have been what she was acting weird about. "Oh, yes. Of course. Yeah, I can't wait." It was wonderful news, so why was McKenzie keeping it to herself?

28

Colt rode with Detective Albrecht to the Phoenix Police Headquarters. He rested his head against the seat, doing his best to keep his scratchy, tired eyes open. He needed sleep, but rest would have to wait.

The sandy-colored, flat-roofed police building reflected its desert location. Colt and Albrecht entered the building on Washington Street and ran into the primary reason the department was getting a new space in a high-rise down the road. People were everywhere. The intake area was jammed with officers processing the overflow of people arrested for their part in the illegal dog fighting operation, which strained the already cramped quarters.

Colt glanced around, wondering how anyone got any work done in this noisy place. "Is Berkley on the job today?"

"I don't know." Albrecht motioned for Colt to follow him as he wound his way to an open workspace. "We'll check his schedule. If he is, I'll call dispatch and find out exactly where he is."

Colt's eyes burned, and he stretched with a yawn. A lot had happened since he last rested his head on a pillow. He wanted to bring this thing with Renegade to a close before he collapsed, and he was almost there. He'd accompany Albrecht to inform Berkley that his step-brother was dead, and he wouldn't leave until he knew the truth of Berkley's involvement. Had the K9 officer set them up in the first place?

Albrecht commandeered a computer at someone's desk in the corner. After his search, he waved Colt closer so he could see. "He's working patrol over in East Lake Park."

"Let's go."

It was barely a five-minute drive, and they found Berkley's cruiser with no trouble. He had parked it outside a Mexican restaurant and came out carrying a breakfast burrito on a paper plate. He saw them pull in behind his unit and held up his free hand in greeting.

Berkley approached Colt's side of the car. "Hey, guys. How's it going?" Colt and Albrecht got out and met Berkley on the sidewalk. His gaze shifted between them. "Is something wrong?"

Albrecht sucked in a deep breath. "Why don't we go back inside and sit down? I could use a cup of coffee."

Colt thought caffeine was an excellent idea, even though he figured Albrecht was using it as an excuse to have Berkley sit down. Maybe he could get some food, as well. "Me too, and the smell of your burrito is making me hungry."

Berkley's eyes narrowed slightly. He knew something was up but went along anyway. "Sure. I have about ten minutes left on my break. How's your wife, Sheriff?"

"Better. We found her dog last night." Colt was far too exhausted to deal with his anger with Caitlyn. They both needed a solid night's sleep before they discussed her reckless behavior during the raid.

The officer's face brightened. "That's really great! I wish I was so lucky."

They chose a table away from the kitchen and other patrons, and after they ordered, Albrecht cleared his throat. "Listen Berkley, we have some bad news. We busted a dogfight last night and, in the mayhem, your stepbrother was shot. I'm sorry to tell you, he didn't survive. He's gone. I'm sorry."

Berkley sat back in his chair and studied them—shock colored his face. "Mel? He was at a dogfight?"

"Yes, that's right."

Berkley's eyes focused on Colt. "Is that where you found your wife's dog?"

Clamping his jaw tight, Colt nodded. "Yeah. Whoever stole him either took him for that purpose or sold him to the people who run those kinds of events."

"Were there a lot of dogs there?"

"Yes. There were two rooms full, and at least fifteen in the storage space where they penned Renegade up."

Berkley swallowed hard and raised his hand to call the server over. "I'm calling off my shift. I need a drink." He ordered two shots of Jack Daniels.

"That's understandable." Albrecht sipped his coffee.

"So, was Mel a spectator, or was he more involved

than that?" Berkley crossed his arms on the table and leaned forward. "Why did he get shot?"

Albrecht answered, "We busted the event with SWAT, but your stepbrother was killed when he tried to attack Deputy Marshal Reed with a knife."

Berkley's brow furrowed in confusion. "Why would he do that?"

The inferno of anger Colt felt when he found out Rankin had attacked Caitlyn surged to a head. "Because first he snuck up behind her and jammed a gun into her back. They were in a secluded room, and since he took the time to unclip her flak jacket to grope her, I'm guessing he thought he might rape her while he was at it. The thing is, Rankin had no clue how capable my wife is. She disarmed him and sent him sprawling. She was holding him at gunpoint when he found his knife and sprang toward her. Caitlyn shot him in self-defense."

Albrecht pressed Colt's arm with a warning hand, and continued, "We're sorry for your loss, but what we want to know is how much of this you were aware of? Did you know that your stepbrother was involved in dogfighting?"

"You're a K9 officer, for God's sake." Colt needed to get a grip. His fury cost him energy he didn't have, and, in the exhaustion, his emotions were out of control.

Berkley held up open hands. "Hey, I didn't know what he was up to. Do you seriously think I would have anything to do with something so barbaric? I love dogs. I asked if you saw the other dogs there because my K9 partner, Axle, has been missing for two months. Were there any other Mals there?"

The server brought Berkley's shots, and he downed

them both, one after the other. Colt's anger dissipated. He believed Berkley. Besides, all the K9 cops he'd ever met were crazy about their dogs. They had to spend too much time with them not to be.

Colt rubbed his eyes with the butt of his palms. "I can't be sure if there were or not, but I didn't see any."

"Christ. It makes me sick to think my own stepbrother would take my dog and force him to fight. But if he stole your wife's dog, he probably took Axle, too." Berkley's eyes dampened, and he ran a hand down over his face. He showed more distress over his dog than his brother which, under the circumstances made sense to Colt.

"The ASPCA confiscated all the dogs at the location." Colt softened his tone. "You can call them to see if they have Axle."

"I will." Berkley shoved his food away. "I feel sick. How did I not see through him? See Mel for the dirtbag he was? Poor Axle. I hate to think what he might have gone through, and after two months... I wonder—is there any way he could survive?"

29

With every mile between Spearfish and home, McKenzie resisted the urge to call Dylan and tell him her incredible news. Her body hummed with excitement that she needed to share. She hoped he wouldn't guard his emotions, like he usually did. In general, her husband was a stoic man on the outside, though she knew in truth his feelings ran deep.

They'd started trying to get pregnant on their wedding night almost a year and a half ago. She had wondered if there was something wrong with one of them, or both. Now, she knew that the only thing wrong was her lack of patience.

Her mind bolted from one topic to the next. First, what would Dylan's reaction be? To whether their baby was a girl or a boy. Where would they set up the nursery? How would she decorate it? Should she go with the traditional blue or pink? Or maybe a neutral? What theme would they choose? Maybe Stella would teach her how to quilt.

McKenzie's stomach interrupted her thoughts with hunger pangs so strong they demanded she eat something right away. There could be no waiting until she got home. She pulled into the Safeway parking lot at the edge of town. As soon as she turned off her engine, she found a baggie with four Saltine crackers and gobbled them like a starved person. That should hold her until she bought some healthy food for a snack on the way back to the ranch.

She purchased some hard-boiled eggs, Triscuits, a snack pack of cut vegetables, and an apple to tide her over until she got home. Before the last on-ramp to the highway, McKenzie pulled into McDonald's and ordered a large chocolate shake, rationalizing that she needed the milk and that all the healthy food would balance out the sugar.

When she arrived at the ranch, Dylan was coming out of the back door from the kitchen. She honked and rolled down the window. "Hi!" That one word packed full of joy was all she had to say.

"It's confirmed? You're pregnant?" Dylan ran to the truck and flung open her door. McKenzie slid from the seat into his arms.

"Yes! Dylan, we're going to have a baby!"

"Do you know if it's a boy or a girl?"

She giggled. "Not yet. We can't find out until I'm four months along. But do we want the doctor to tell us, or should we wait?"

"I want to know!"

"What are you hoping for?" She figured he'd want a son.

"Healthy." He lifted her gently from the ground and turned her around as he kissed her tenderly. "What do you want?"

"I don't think I care, but I picture a boy."

"When are you due?"

"May 21st."

"May. My grandma's birthday was in May." He squeezed her. "Let's go tell my folks!" He set her carefully on her feet as though she might break.

"I was thinking maybe we should keep this to ourselves until the end of the first trimester."

"Why?" His expression told her how crazy he thought her idea was. "I can't wait to shout it from the mountaintops."

McKenzie's heart swelled at seeing how proud he was. "I do too, but I also want it to be a little secret for us to share for just a couple of weeks."

The gleam in Dylan's eyes softened, and he touched her cheek with his rough fingers. "Alright. If that's what you want, I'll wait. But when we decide to make the announcement, look out!"

"Deal." She wrapped her arms around his waist. "There's another reason I want to stall a little. I don't want everyone to be all excited about a new baby when Caitlyn and Colt come home. I'd hate to cause them any more pain."

Dylan kissed the top of her head. "You're always

thinking of others. It's one of the reasons I love you so much. I agree. Let's give them some time."

"Oh! I almost forgot to tell you. I spoke with Caitlyn on the way home. They found Renegade! She was with him at an emergency vet clinic when she called."

"That's great news. Where did they find him?"

"At a dogfight. He has some injuries, but they should heal up quickly. Doctor Moore is consulting with the vet in Phoenix, and they'll determine if Renegade can travel home or if he should stay in Arizona for wound care."

"I bet Caitlyn is over the moon."

"She is. It was so good to hear an upbeat tone in her voice. She's been through so much in the past several days."

Dylan reached into the truck and turned the power on, then scrolled through a playlist on his phone. *Who I Am with You* by Chris Young vibrated through the speakers and Dylan took her hand. Twirling her, he spun her into him so that her back was to his chest. He wrapped his arms around her and swayed with her to the rhythm of the country western sound.

Jace ran out of the kitchen, letting the screen door bang behind him. "Hi, Aunt Kenzie!" he yelled, holding up a gallon-sized zipper bag filled with cookies. "Look what Grandma gave us to take when we go back out to the fences, Uncle Dylan!"

Stella stuck her head out the door. "Jace! Don't let the screen slam behind you like that when you go outside."

"Sorry, Grandma!" he called over his shoulder, though his tone held no remorse as he ran up to them. "Chocolate chocolate-chip!"

Dylan gave him a stern look, though merriment danced in his eyes. "I believe the answer you meant to give your grandmother is 'Yes, ma'am.'"

Jace's eyes widened, and he turned around. "Yes, ma'am, Grandma. And thanks for the cookies!"

Stella couldn't keep from laughing as she followed her grandson. "You two look like you're awfully happy about something. Dancing in the driveway in the middle of the day? What's going on?"

Dylan's body straightened, and he took an excited breath, but McKenzie nudged him in the ribs to remind him they were keeping their pregnancy a secret, even from his mother.

"I talked to Caitlyn this morning. She said they found Renegade."

Stella covered her mouth with her hand, and her eyes moistened. "Is he okay?"

"He will be."

"That's such good news. I'm so relieved. My poor girl has already lost too much. When are they coming home?"

"As soon as the vet says Renegade is safe to travel. I'm sure they'll be back in Wyoming in a day or two."

"I'll make Caitlyn her favorite chocolate cake." Stella stopped at the gate and tilted her head. "So, you two were dancing because of Renegade?"

Dylan looked away. He never could lie to his mother's face, and McKenzie tried her best to evade the question. "That and because you made chocolate chocolate-chip cookies."

A sly, knowing smile plumped her mother-in-law's

cheeks. "Yes. Cookies are always good news. I'm so happy you have them."

30

———

Caitlyn and Renegade were curled up together, asleep on one of the two beds in their hotel room, when Colt finally got back from his and Albrecht's meeting with Officer Berkley. Normally, his wife never let her dog sleep on the furniture. But after the hell they'd gone through, he was glad to see them resting in the comfort of one another.

He leaned against the desk and watched them. His emotions ranged from gratitude and joy, to an unspeakable sorrow, to white-hot anger. Despite his fatigue Colt was too keyed up to sleep, so he changed into his gym clothes and left the gently snoring pair to rest while he beat his stress and rollercoaster feelings into submission. Only then would he be able to truly rest, and he had to have a clear head before he talked with Caitlyn about her actions during the raid.

Bright lights lit the hotel exercise room, but it lacked a decent selection of weights, but he used what he could before he programmed the treadmill for a run. He sprinted for twenty minutes, sweating out his tension, before his body faltered. Exhaustion finally won the battle, and he set the machine to the cool-down pace. After stretching, he gulped down two bottles of water and went back to the room.

Caitlyn was still in a deep sleep, so he kept the lights off, ordered a meat-lover's pizza for delivery, and took a blistering hot shower. Once his body was as energy depleted as he could get it, he was ready for a snooze.

When his food came, he set himself up on the second bed and turned on the TV with the sound muted. He watched the news as he inhaled three cheesy slices, slowing down on the fourth. If Caitlyn woke up later, she could reheat some for her supper in the room's microwave.

Colt fell asleep with the TV on but woke again several hours later to the oven's beeping alert and the smell of melted mozzarella. Caitlyn ran to stop the sound before she pulled out some pizza she'd plated on a torn off section of the pizza box.

She grimaced. "Sorry to wake you." She sat cross-legged on the end of his bed.

"That's okay." Colt rubbed his eyes and pushed himself up to sit against the headboard. "How are you feeling? Did you get some good rest? You and Ren were asleep when I got back." He fumbled with the alarm clock to check the time. "It's only 2:00 a.m."

"I think we fell asleep yesterday afternoon around 3:30. Ren woke me about ten minutes ago, wanting me to take him out." Her dog was back on the bed with his nose resting between his front paws, but his alert eyes watched them.

"You got almost twelve hours, then. That's good. You needed it." Colt reached for the bottle of water he left on the shelf table between the beds. "Do you think you'll be able to go back to sleep after you eat?"

Caitlyn shrugged. "I'm still tired, so we'll see. But, if you're up for it, I'd like to talk. We didn't leave things very well yesterday."

"No, we didn't, but honestly, I'd rather get more rest before we talk. I'm still worn out, and I don't want to say anything I don't mean."

A spark of heat ignited in Caitlyn's amber eyes, which was a definite warning to him. "You're so angry with me you think you'll say things you don't mean?"

"Catie, that's not what I said. I said, I'm exhausted. Can we please do this in the morning?" The anger he was hoping to avoid roiled in the pit of his belly.

"Sure, but we have to leave early. I booked us on the first flight out."

"Did the vet clear Renegade to travel?"

"Yeah. Doctor Moore advised against surgery, and so the vet here cleaned and bandaged his wounds and gave him a thorough check over. I'll take him to see Doctor Moore when we get home, and he can set up a care protocol." Caitlyn took a bite of her pizza. A long string of cheese hung between the slice and her teeth when she pulled it from her mouth. She laughed around her bite.

The cheerful sound soothed the crispy edges of Colt's agitation. He realized she hadn't laughed since before their collision. His emotions were still askew, and he rubbed his face with both hands, trying to wipe all the feelings away. In one moment, he imagined taking Caitlyn by the shoulders, shaking her hard, and yelling at her for her dangerous behavior. In the next, he wanted to pull her onto his lap and cradle her until all her pain went away. And sometimes he wanted to throw her onto the bed and overcome her stubbornness, physically showing her all the intensity she stirred in him.

Instead, he swallowed his soup of anxious thoughts. "I bet you're still hungry. Do you want more pizza?"

"I'll get it." Caitlyn slid off the bed. Her K9 Trials T-shirt barely covered her backside and when she reached up to heat another slice, the view she offered him made him bite his lip. He rolled over and buried his face in his pillow. If he made love to his wife right now, it would confuse things. She would believe everything was fine between them. And it was not.

The next thing he knew, Caitlyn was gently nudging his shoulder. "Hey, sleepyhead. Time to get up. We've got to get going."

He pushed himself up from the mattress and saw that Caitlyn and Renegade were packed and ready to leave. "I need a quick shower."

"No problem."

"It would have been nice to have some time to talk this morning."

Irritation colored her tone. "It can wait until we get home. Can't it?"

"I guess it's going to have to." Colt padded to the bathroom.

CAITLYN WATCHED him stride across the room. She was glad they didn't have time to talk and since she reserved the flight on such short notice, their seats weren't together on the plane. A confrontation with Colt was the last thing she needed right now. Her head was killing her, and she was barely hanging on to stability as it was.

All Caitlyn wanted was to get home, go on a run on the mountain path that circled her property, and sleep another full night. Of course, she couldn't run because of her concussion, but she'd at least go on a long walk through the woods. Maybe then she'd be ready to discuss the raid with Colt. At the moment, she was still furious at him for calling her out in front of the other cops. He wasn't her dad, after all. Or even her boss.

On some deep-down level, Caitlyn knew she was using anger to keep more painful emotions at bay. It was easier to be mad at Colt than to face the loss of their baby and the truth of her impetuous decisions. She pasted on as much of a smile as she could construct and hollered to Colt in the bathroom that she was going to load their things in the car. "I'll check us out of our room at the front desk, and Ren and I will wait for you in the lobby."

31

I t was good to be back in Wyoming riding in her own K9 vehicle, with Renegade stretched out comfortably in the kennel. She dozed on the long ride home from the Rapid City Airport in South Dakota, which pushed her impending conversation with Colt farther out. She wanted to work things out with him, but instinctively she resisted the idea of dredging through her emotional swamp. Facing the depths of her pain was too much to deal with right then. Caitlyn only wanted to focus on the good news that she'd found Ren. The rest she would keep tucked inside until she was ready to deal with it, one thing at a time.

A nap would also bolster her reserves in preparation for seeing her family. She understood they wanted to comfort her, and even though she'd rather be left alone, she would make the expected appearance at the ranch and accept their love and all the kind, well-intended words. She felt guilty not wanting to see them. But their genuine love and acceptance would make staying in control of her shaky emotional state an impossibility.

When she woke from her nap, Caitlyn glanced at Colt, who had insisted on driving. "I wish we could just go to our house."

"I know, me too. But we're going into Moose Creek so Doctor Moore can look at Renegade's injuries, anyway, and your mom has already made us a welcome home dinner."

"There's no doubt about that." Caitlyn forced a smile as she rested her throbbing head against the door. "At least most of the bruising on my face has faded. I hate when she fusses over me like I'm a China doll."

"She loves you. And though you like to forget it, you *are* her only daughter."

"I suppose," she chuffed. "Did I tell you that Athena is pregnant with Ren's litter?"

"No." Colt's face brightened. Obviously, they could both use some good news.

"Sorry. With everything going on, I forgot to mention it. I found out when I spoke with Doctor Moore about Renegade's care."

"That's exciting. I bet it makes you happy."

"I'm thrilled. But it's weird that McKenzie didn't tell me, herself. You'd think she would have told me as soon as she found out."

"Well, maybe she figured you were dealing with a lot at the time."

"I suppose. But it seems like she's acting distant lately."

"You might be oversensitive right now. I wouldn't

worry about it, but if it's bugging you, you should ask her."

They crested the hill before rolling down onto Moose Creek's Main Street. The familiar scene comforted her in a way no words could. They parked in the dirt lot behind the vet clinic. Doctor Moore stepped out the rear door as they got out of the car.

"It sure is good to have you both home safe and sound." Dr. Moore shook Colt's hand and hugged Caitlyn. "How's our patient?"

"Looks like he's happy to see you." Renegade sat in the car kennel, wagging his tail and barking. Caitlyn opened the side door and helped him out. "His leg is still very sore. He doesn't like to put weight on it if he doesn't have to."

Doctor Moore watched Renegade walk, favoring the bandaged leg. "Let's take him inside. Colt, why don't you carry him, to save him from walking on it?"

Caitlyn reached for her dog. "I'll get him."

Colt beat her to Ren, murmuring, "You know you're not supposed to be lifting anything for a couple of weeks after your procedure. You've been way over doing it, Catie. Just let me help."

Caitlyn glowered at Colt. She hated being treated with kid gloves as though she were a fainting violet. Her regular training included carrying Renegade on her shoulder and she could easily do it better than Colt. Her tongue itched to tell him so, but she didn't want to start an argument in front of the veterinarian. Besides, she knew he was right.

"Accepting help doesn't mean you're weak, Catie."

Colt brushed his fingers over her cheek and the sweetness of touch made her heart ache. She clamped her teeth together and forced her precarious emotions to stay pushed down deep. Caitlyn was on the brink of falling apart and she couldn't allow that to happen. Not here. Not now.

Doctor Moore gave Renegade an overall exam and then, with a soft touch, unwrapped the bandaging around Renegade's foreleg. "This looks to be healing nicely. I see no obvious signs of infection, but you will want to keep him on his antibiotic until he finishes the prescription."

"Got it." Caitlyn stroked Renegade's silky head, and he licked her hand.

"I imagine you both will be taking it easy for the next week or so."

"That's what everyone tells me," Caitlyn said with a sigh.

The veterinarian squeezed her shoulder. "I realize resting doesn't come naturally to either you or Renegade, but if you behave, you'll both be back on your feet faster if you do."

Colt laughed softly. "Got any horse tranquilizers I can use on them this week, Doc?"

After they finished at the vet clinic, Colt drove them out to the Reeds' ranch. Her mother was waiting on the porch when they pulled up and she hurried down the steps as they parked.

"It's so good to see the three of you." Stella made her way to Caitlyn's side of the car and embraced her, and

Caitlyn did her best to relax and not pull away. "Is there anything I can carry? How can I help?"

"I'm fine, Ma. Really." Caitlyn shifted so she could let Renegade out of the back. "Thanks for cooking us dinner." She helped Ren ease himself onto the ground. "Once he's on the floor, he gets around pretty good." Her dog wagged his tail and greeted Stella with a sloppy dog kiss.

"Good boy, Renegade." Stella crouched down and stroked both sides of his face. "John and McKenzie made a comfy bed for you to rest on, and they set it right in front of the fire." Renegade licked her cheek.

Colt came around the hood and, after kissing the dry side of Stella's face, he hugged her tight. "Thanks for all of this, Stella. How's Jace been? I hope he minded his manners."

"Colt, that boy is just like you. It makes me feel like I'm in my thirties again having him here." She patted his arm.

At that moment, a speeding gray streak zipped by, chased by a racing boy. "Hi Dad!" Jace came to a skidding halt next to Caitlyn, and wrapping a dirty arm around her waist, he squeezed. "Hi Caitlyn, I'm sorry you got hurt in a car wreck. I'm really glad you're okay."

Warm gratitude flowed through her, and she bent to hug him. His simple unassuming statements were a relief. "Thank you, Jace. That's sweet."

Colt searched over his shoulder for the mysterious flash. "What just ran by us?"

"Oh, that was Storm. He's my dog."

"*Your* dog?" Colt looked askance toward Stella.

She held up her hands. "Don't look at me. Talk to Dylan and McKenzie. I had nothing to do with it." She laughed, and with an arm around Caitlyn's waist, she led them all into the house.

Caitlyn breathed in the comforting aroma of dinner cooking mingled with the fire blazing in the hearth. Her dad strode across the room and drew her into a suffocating bear hug. Emotion welled up, and she held onto him, soaking the front of his flannel shirt with tears she could not hold back. When she pulled herself together enough to face the others, she let him go.

Tilting her chin up, her father's dark eyes searched her matching ones. "You're gonna hurt for a while, darlin'. But you're strong. So is Renegade. You two will get back on your feet, but you've got to give it time."

"Thanks, Dad." Caitlyn glanced at her brother and McKenzie who were standing by the fireplace holding hands and glancing at each other nervously. She wiped her eyes on her sleeve and studied them. Colt shook John's hand, but then John pulled him into a back-clapping man hug.

Caitlyn crossed the carpet to embrace Dylan. "What is going on with you two?"

"What do you mean?" Dylan held on to her a little longer than usual.

Colt approached him and shoved her brother's arm. "Did you say Jace could have a dog?"

"A dog? No... I didn't say that. The dog chose him. They picked each other. What was I supposed to do?"

Dylan laughed and glanced at McKenzie, who shrugged. "He said that Jace could have a horse, though.

And he swore to me you would be fine with it and that you would agree with him it was necessary on a ranch."

Caitlyn shifted her gaze to Colt to gauge his reaction. Colt had grown up on the Reed ranch, but her dad had never given him a horse of his own. Would he think the gift was too much? Colt's expression remained passive, but the tips of his ears turned red. He was already holding a lot of feelings in. It was time to change the subject.

"What's for dinner, Ma? It smells so good. I've been too busy to eat much in the past couple of days, and I could inhale an entire pot of whatever you've got simmering in the kitchen." Caitlyn was grateful for the love her mom showered on her. She felt safe and accepted here at her childhood home. Still, she couldn't afford to relax her ironclad grip on her emotions. She'd almost dissolved in them when her dad had held her close, but if she let go now, she would drown in the ocean's depth of them.

Stella beamed with pleasure. Nothing made Caitlyn's mom happier than feeding her people with comfort food designed to cure what ailed. "Chicken and Dumplings. And I baked your favorite chocolate cake for dessert."

Colt took the cue and followed Caitlyn to the table. "Jace, go wash up for dinner, son. Then you can tell us all about what you did on the ranch while we were away."

The family took their spots at the long table, and Colt leaned around Caitlyn to speak to Dylan. "Hey, Dyl. Thanks for your generosity. I agree a horse is necessary on the ranch. But in the future, I'd prefer you to talk to me about major gifts like that. I think Jace should have to *earn* his horse. Don't you?"

Dylan's broad smile brightened his eyes. "I certainly do. Let's come up with a plan for that. I'll go with whatever you decide. And I'll tell you what else. I think *you've* earned the right to have your own horse here, too. It's time you stopped having to borrow your wife's old nag. How 'bout tomorrow you come out and choose one from the herd I brought home from the auction? There are a couple of nice mounts in there."

"Old nag?" Caitlyn said with indignation. "Whiskey is no old nag. He could still outrun Sampson any day of the week," she argued in good nature, grateful for her brother's teasing way.

"Is that a challenge? You're on little sister. Any time, any day."

With that, the family fell into an easy conversation, punctuated by Jace's questions and nonsensical stories. It was good to be home among the people who knew her best and who respected she needed to just *be* for a while before she talked about everything that happened in Arizona.

Caitlyn's phone vibrated in her hip pocket. She glanced at the screen. "I should probably take this." She pushed away from the table and went to stand by the fire. "Hi Blake. What's up?"

The doctor's deep, rich voice flowed through the speaker. "Hey. How are you feeling? Are you home?"

"Yeah, we're having dinner at my folks' place. I'm fine. A little weak, I guess."

"That's to be expected. How's your head?"

"It hurts."

"Any dizziness, or severe headaches?"

"Not today."

"And how are you doing emotionally?"

"I'll be fine."

"I know you will, but until you are… talk to me about what you're feeling."

Caitlyn sighed. "I'm sad, of course. But we found Ren, and we're home. So that makes things better."

"That's great news about your dog, and I'm glad you're doing better, but I'd like you to set up an appointment with your therapist."

"I have to anyway, in order to get clearance to go back to work. I was involved in a shooting."

"Oh, Caitlyn. I'm sorry. You've had a hell of a time."

"It's all good." She could not talk about how hellish the time had been. Not yet. Not now.

"No, it's not. The only good thing is that you're safe, and that you found Renegade. I'd like to see you for a quick checkup so I can see for myself how you truly are. Are you free tomorrow?"

"I can be." Stella gestured to gain her attention and Caitlyn covered the phone with her hand. Her mom mouthed, *Thanksgiving,* and Caitlyn gave her a thumbs up. "My mom wants to know if you want to come out to the ranch for Thanksgiving?"

Blake hesitated. "That's so kind, and I would have really loved to be there. Unfortunately, I just made plans to be in Jackson Hole for the holiday."

"No worries."

"I hope I'll get an invitation again next year. I'm

honestly bummed that I'm already booked. I would have rather spent Thanksgiving there with you. With your family."

"You have an open invitation to come here anytime you want, you know that." Colt sent her a look that hardened at the corners of his eyes, so she quickly amended. "My *mom* always loves when you visit."

"I'll count on it, then. Next year—Thanksgiving at the Reeds'."

"Sounds good."

"I'll see you tomorrow, then?"

Caitlyn sighed. "Yes. I'll be there."

32

———————

The following morning, McKenzie loaded the two pit bulls she was watching into crates in the bed of Dylan's F350. It was time for their vet check. Storm seemed sullen. Perhaps he was already missing Jace since the boy went home with Caitlyn and his dad last night. Truth be told, she missed him, too.

She pressed her palm against her abdomen and smiled. One day soon, she'd have her own little person who never had to go away... at least not until college. McKenzie laughed at how far she was getting ahead of herself.

The drive to town was only slightly over forty-five minutes, but by the time she got there, she was starving. It was ridiculous how ravenous she'd become. The little one inside must have an enormous appetite, but McKenzie didn't have time to stop for anything until after her appointment with Doctor Moore.

She leashed the dogs before they hopped out of the bed of the truck. When she was halfway through the parking area, a horn beeped two times, and she turned to see Caitlyn waving from her Explorer.

Her friend pulled into the lot and rolled down her window. "Hey! Look at these two gorgeous babies." Caitlyn smiled at the dogs and stretched her hand out of her car for them to sniff. "They sure look healthy and happy, Kenzie. You've done a great job with them in the past week."

"I think they're relieved to have a safe, comfortable home and plenty of food. It's amazing how dogs will respond to a little care and kindness. Storm thought he found himself a best friend, and he's been mopey today since Jace is no longer at the ranch."

"That's so sweet. A boy and his dog."

"Did Colt say anything? I mean, about Jace keeping Storm?"

"No, I think Colt was more concerned about the horse." Caitlyn shifted her car into park. "Hold on, I'll come in with you. I'm super early for my appointment with Blake. I was going to grab a cup of coffee and a cinnamon roll from the café before I went to the clinic."

"That sounds so good right now, I can't even tell you."

The women walked side by side, and Caitlyn took Storm's leash. "He's so much more docile than he was when I first saw him, but I don't know how he'd get along with Renegade. Their original meeting didn't go well, and Ren isn't one to forget." She opened the door to the vet's office and waited for McKenzie to enter. "Besides, now isn't a good time to force Renegade to deal with another dog. He has a lot more healing to do—emotionally and physically."

With a heavy heart, McKenzie agreed. "You're right, of course. But maybe Colt will let us keep Storm at the ranch for Jace. That way Storm would have one home instead of two and he couldn't upset Ren."

"That sounds like a good idea to me. At least for now. How does Storm get along with Larry, Athena, and Ember?"

McKenzie grinned. "Larry ignores him, and so far, Storm has been a gentleman with the girls. It's almost as though he knows he'd better behave if he wants to keep this new cushy life."

The rescue dogs both got a clean bill of health from Doctor Moore, and McKenzie returned them to their kennels in the truck. She and Caitlyn crossed the street to the café to order breakfast.

McKenzie studied the menu. "Everything looks so good. I'm thinking of ordering the Big-Rancher combo and French toast."

Caitlyn's eyebrows shot up, but she said nothing.

"Has your mom talked with you about Thanksgiving?" McKenzie set her menu on the table and waved to let Stephanie know they were ready to order.

"Yeah, she asked me to bring the relishes. Does she think I can't cook or something?"

McKenzie giggled, knowing that though Caitlyn had a lot of talents, cooking was not one of them. "She probably just wants to give you a break. You've been through so much lately."

"I guess." Caitlyn didn't look like she bought that line. "Colt is a pretty decent cook. We could bring something more."

"Did your mom tell you Logan and Addison are coming up for the weekend?"

"Yes, and I can't wait. It'll be so good to see them. I miss Logan now that he lives down in Denver."

"Are you going hunting with your dad and brothers on Black Friday?"

"I want to, but no shooting for me until my head heals. Colt is taking Jace, though. It'll be his first time. You ought to go with them."

"I don't know…"

"Talk to Dyl about it. I bet he'd love it if you came. Then you and Jace could both learn together."

McKenzie declined the coffee Stephanie brought. "I'll just have water. Thank you."

Stephanie filled Caitlyn's cup. "You ladies ready to order?"

McKenzie's stomach roared loud enough for all three of them to hear. They laughed and McKenzie said, "I guess I better order first. I was going to have the Big Rancher, but suddenly the thought of fried eggs makes me feel queasy. How about biscuits and gravy with a side of bacon and a bowl of fruit?" She pursed her lips. "Does that come with pancakes?"

Stephanie grinned at her. "It can—if you want. You sure are hungry this morning. Babysitting a ten-year-old must have really taken its toll!"

"He is a bundle of energy, that's for sure." McKenzie was grateful that Stephanie came up with her own reasons for the huge breakfast order.

She waited until Steph filled Caitlyn's coffee mug and took her cinnamon roll order. As soon as Stephanie left,

McKenzie asked, "Did you know your parents are planning a trip to Malta?"

"What? I wasn't gone that long, but it feels like I missed a ton. When did they decide that? Where is Malta, by the way?"

"It's in the middle of the Mediterranean Sea, off the tip of the boot of Italy."

"Why on earth did they choose to go there?"

"Who knows? It's like they're twenty-something again and want some grand adventures."

"I guess it makes sense. My mom was so young when they got married and had Dylan. After that, there was no time or money for anything but the ranch."

"I say, good for them."

"Me too." Caitlyn raised her mug and clinked against McKenzie's water glass.

Breakfast arrived, and McKenzie's feast took up half the table. She couldn't wait to dig in. Caitlyn's solitary cinnamon roll looked small and lonely on her side. McKenzie cut into the edge of one of the fluffy home-made biscuits swamped with gravy.

"So, why are you seeing Blake this morning? Didn't you get the stamp of health by the doctors in Phoenix?"

"I have to have my blood drawn every week for a month to make sure the pregnancy hormone is receding. I guess there's a risk of an ectopic pregnancy."

"What's that?"

"When an egg attaches somewhere outside of the uterus. I don't have that. My hormone levels already were going down. They just want to be safe, and you know how Blake is. He's such a worry-wort."

"I'm so sorry, Caitlyn." McKenzie reached across the table and gripped her friend's hand. "For everything."

"I know. Me too—but life goes on." Caitlyn peeled a chunk of cinnamony dough from her pastry and hesitated before asking, "McKenzie, why didn't you tell me about Athena's pregnancy? I had to hear that she was expecting puppies from Doctor Moore."

McKenzie choked on a piece of bacon. "I... I just figured you didn't need anything else to worry about."

"But it's great news. I'm thrilled."

"But, with all you were dealing with..."

Caitlyn set her fork on her plate. The corners of her mouth pulled downward, and she chuffed, "I'm not a cream puff, Kenze." Then her features softened again. "I never want you to feel you can't tell me something. No matter what. That's what best friends... sisters... are for."

Guilt clogged McKenzie's throat, and she suddenly felt like she was going to be sick. "I know." She squeezed Caitlyn's hand as she slid out of the booth. "I'll be right back."

33

Colt and Jace drove out to the ranch first thing in the morning. Dylan had already picked a horse he thought was perfect for Jace, but Colt got to choose his own. It was silly how excited he was. He'd always wanted a horse of his own, but it had never come up and he never had the courage to ask. Now, after all these years, it was a dream come true.

When they got there, Dylan was working a small gelding in the round pen and John stood by, watching. Colt and Jace climbed up to sit on the top rail.

Jace waved. "Hi Grandpa!"

John's eyes gleamed with pleasure. The boy gave the older man new life. Jace leaned into Colt and whispered, "Do you think that's gonna be my horse?"

Colt warmed at the marvel and excitement he witnessed in his son's eyes. "I don't know. I've never seen this horse before, but Uncle Dylan said he brought a bunch home. This fella could be any of those."

"Mornin'," Dylan called from the center of the circle without breaking his focus on the horse.

"Nice looking horse." Colt braced his elbows on his knees. "One of your new ones?"

"Yep. This is the guy I think will be perfect for you, Jace. What do you think of him?"

"Really?" Jace's face split in half with his wide, toothy grin.

"Really. But only if you take good care of him."

John walked over and placed a hand on Jace's back. "You know, your horse must come first on a ranch. Before breakfast. Before the dogs. And usually before the sun."

"I'll take care of him! I swear!" Jace's face went from beaming to cloudy in a flash. "But what about the days I'm not here?"

"I've been thinking about that." Dylan twirled the end of a long rope to keep the horse moving around the pen. "I could take care of him for you on those days, but you'd have to do something for me in return."

"I'll do whatever you want!" The sunshine was back.

"There's a lot of work needs doing 'round here. And mucking stalls is one job that never goes away. So, when you're here, after you feed and water your horse, you'll be responsible for cleaning out all the stalls in the barn and raking the runs."

Jace appeared to be considering this offer, and Colt hid a grin behind his hand. The boy's head bobbed slowly up and down. "Okay. That's a lot of poop, but it's a deal." He spat in his palm and held it out to Dylan.

Dylan's eyebrows shot up, and he chuckled. After bringing the gelding to a halt, he strode over to his nephew and shook his moist hand. "Done. You'll have to think of a name for him."

"I get to name him?" Jace jumped down from the rail, but before he could run toward the horse, Dylan caught him by the waist with his arm.

"Whoa, little dude. What do you know about running around the horses?"

"Not to. I'm sorry."

"I know you're excited, and you should be. But you have to be a good leader for your horse and stay calm. Go say hello, but then we're going out to the paddock. Your dad needs to choose a horse today, too."

Jace slowly approached his new gelding, holding his hand out like he would if he were greeting a dog. The horse backed away. "I don't think he likes me."

"He doesn't know you." Dylan leaned against the rail next to Colt.

John rested his hands on his hips. "Be patient. He's curious, and he'll come up to you when he's ready."

It took about five minutes, but finally the little Quarter Horse took one step toward Jace, and then another. He approached the boy with a nicker, and Jace gently stroked the horse's flat cheek. Turning bright eyes to Colt, John, and Dylan, he said, "I think his name is Rusty."

After giving Jace and the horse a while to bond, John went up to the house and the rest of them walked down to the paddock behind the barn. Seven horses milled about in the pen. Dylan threw half a bale of hay out into the middle, and they watched as the small herd jockeyed for their share. A beautiful black horse with one white sock pinned his ears back and strode to the center of the pile. Standing over it, he ate what he pleased. Meanwhile, three other horses bucked, kicked, and nipped at each other, determining who would be second, and so on. The remaining horses ran circles around the more aggressive steeds, waiting until the dominant horses were done. In this case, if Dylan didn't toss out more hay, they'd go without.

"So," Dylan reached to the ground and pulled up a long, dry strand of grass and chewed the end. "What do you think?"

Colt grinned. "You know what I think."

"Yeah," Dylan's voice tripped on his laugh. "I suppose I do. What'll you name him?"

"He's gorgeous, Dyl. Is he really for me?"

"You sound like your son."

"I feel like he does." A lump formed in Colt's throat, and he coughed it away. "Remember in fourth grade, when Mrs. Walker read us that book about the black stallion?"

"Uh, sort of. Maybe."

"I remember because I wanted a horse like that so badly. It probably wasn't a big deal to you, since you had a barn full of horses already. Anyway, that horse was called Shetahn. I think I'll name him that after my first imaginary horse all those years ago."

"Good God, you sound more like Caitlyn every day," Dylan teased. "But it's as good a name as any, I suppose. Go get him... if you can." Laughing, he handed Colt a halter. He clapped a hand on Jace's neck, steering him back toward the round pen and Rusty.

Colt found a lead rope and strode out to the middle of the herd. The black horse raised his head to look at him and then went back to eating. With steady, certain movement, Colt looped the rope around the horse's neck and then slid the halter over his face. Once he had it buckled, Colt allowed the horse to eat more while he stroked his long, powerful neck. "Good to meet you, Shetahn. I think I'll call you Tahn, for short."

When the hay was gone, Colt led his new horse out to the arena where Dylan was teaching Jace how to groom and tack. "What are your plans for the rest of those horses?"

Dylan grinned. "Well, I'll keep the calmest one for our own little guy, and probably train up the rest and sell them."

"What little guy?" Colt frowned in question.

Dylan's eyes popped, and he stuttered. "I, uh. Nothing. That's not what I meant. Never mind." His face above his beard reddened.

"What?" Colt cocked his head. "What little guy, Dylan?"

Dylan's voice dropped to a harsh whisper. "Be quiet. You're gonna get me killed."

Colt looped the lead rope around the area rail and joined them in the center. "What the hell are you talking about?"

"Can't you just drop it?" Dylan glanced at the house.

Sudden comprehension dawned on Colt, and he whispered, "You and McKenzie are having a little guy?"

"Oh, for God's sake, Colt. Shut up."

A slow smile formed on Colt's lips. "Congratulations,

man. Why the hell do we have to be quiet about it? We should be celebrating."

Dylan closed his eyes and rolled his bottom lip in between his teeth, just like Caitlyn always did. "We want to keep it to ourselves for a little while. Listen, Colt. You cannot tell Caitlyn."

Colt held up both hands. "Oh, no. You can't ask that of me. Do you know how much trouble I'd be in if I knew and said nothing to her? No way, man. I won't tell your folks, or anyone else, if you don't want. But I'm not keeping anything from Catie." They were having a hard enough time without him adding secrets to the mix.

"Damn it, Colt. I didn't mean to say that. I'm gonna be in far more trouble than you."

Jace's freckled nose tilted up, and he squinted with one eye. "What are you guys talking about?"

"Nothing," both men said in unison.

He shrugged and stroked Rusty's nose. "Dad? I know I can't live out here on the ranch all the time, but do you think I could live with you and Caitlyn every day instead of just sometimes?"

Colt's chest squeezed tight against his lungs, and he swallowed hard. "That's not up to me, buddy. I can talk to your mom about the schedule, but she'd miss you if you didn't stay with her half the time, too. I have some good news, though. You get to be with us for both Thanksgiving *and* Christmas! And even better—we'll be out here at the ranch for those holidays, so you can hang out with Rusty and Storm."

"See." Jace kicked the dirt. "Mom doesn't even want me around for Christmas." Jace's comment tore Colt's heart out. "Can I at least bring Storm to live at your house when I'm there?"

"Oh, buddy. I don't know. It all depends on Renegade, and I don't think Catie will want to do anything that makes him anxious right now. They've both had a hard time."

Dylan chucked the boy's chin. "Don't worry, Storm has a place here as long as he needs one. And knowing my sister, if he and Ren can learn to be friends, you'll get to take him home before you know it."

34

Caitlyn left McKenzie at the café and drove to her appointment at the clinic with Blake... Doctor Kennedy. It was always weird for her to think of a man whom she had once had feelings for in a professional, clinical way. But he was the only doctor in their little town, and she trusted him, so she'd grin and bear it.

She and Blake had been dating when Colt first came back on the scene and swept her off her feet. She'd loved Colt as long as she could remember. They'd grown up together, and she'd had a crush on him back when he was just Logan and Dylan's friend. Then, in high school, they fell in love and became serious too fast. He was her first love—her first everything.

She still remembered the crushing pain she felt the day after graduation when Colt came to her house, hat in hand, and confessed that during a drunken night at a graduation party, he'd slept with Allison Snow. He begged her for forgiveness, but Caitlyn had told him to go to hell.

It took years for her to forgive him, but she eventually did. And even though she was dating Blake, and really cared for him, when Colt risked declaring his love for her in a cramped interview room at the courthouse, she couldn't deny her feelings for him any longer, and she broke Blake's heart.

Blake was a good guy, though—a true gentleman—and had become a friend to them both. Well, maybe the term *friend* was too strong for how Colt felt about him, but Blake had saved Colt's life when he got shot, and so her husband tolerated the man.

Caitlyn checked in at the clinic and the receptionist showed her to an exam room. She sat on the paper covering the table to wait. There was a gentle knock, and the doorknob turned. Blake, with his movie-star looks, peered through the opening. His bright blue eyes searched hers.

THERE SHE WAS, in living color, even more beautiful than in his thoughts. Blake's heart rate doubled, and he drew in a calming breath through his nose. "Caitlyn. God, it's good to see you." He reached for her hand, but instead of a professional shake, he clasped on to it. Too long—obviously—he could tell by the way she pulled her fingers away from his. "How are you feeling?" he asked feebly, knowing how she would answer. "And don't give me 'I'm fine'. I want to know the truth."

CAITLYN MET BLAKE'S BRIGHT, crystalline eyes after they'd scanned her from head to toe when he asked how she was. He held up his hand as if to stop her from speaking, and his gold monogrammed cufflinks flashed in the light. No one else in Moose Creek ever wore cufflinks.

She noticed how crisp and ultra-white his collar was against his neck, and that his inky colored hair looked freshly cut. He was so different from Colt and her brothers. Blake had none of their ruggedness, and they didn't have any of his smooth flare. She had often wondered if the big-city doctor would last in their tiny mountain town. But he was still there.

THE SMALL SMILE that curled up on the right side of her mouth wormed its way into his heart. "Okay. I'm *not* fine." Her cheeks blossomed. "But I will be."

He wanted to hold her. To comfort her. "Any pain? Cramping?" Blake sat across from her on a wheeled stool and brought up her medical file on the computer.

"Yes. I've had some cramping, but it seems to be easing up."

"Bleeding?"

"That's pretty much over with." The paper rattled underneath her as she fidgeted on the table. "You're not planning to give me a physical exam, are you?" Her voice crackled with sudden panic.

"No. Other than to check your vitals. I also want to

look at your eyes. You sustained a serious concussion and then proceeded to chase down violent criminals. How are your headaches?"

"Constant. Sometimes better, sometimes worse."

Blake let his breath out slowly. He knew Caitlyn well enough not to lecture her. "Resting should help that. Have you had much nausea?"

"Yes, but since I've been home, that seems better."

"Good. Following the concussion protocol is important. You'll heal faster if you do."

"I know. But I had to find Renegade, Blake. You get that, right?"

"I do. But now that you're home, please take it easy."

"I'll try."

He smiled at her resigned tone. "Mostly, I just want to talk to you, today. I needed to see you with my own eyes to be sure you were okay. How are you doing emotionally?" He touched her knee, letting his fingers rest there. "You've experienced a true loss. One you will grieve. Don't let that surprise you."

BLAKE WANTED to talk to her about her feelings, which was the last thing she was prepared to do. He placed his hand on her knee, and his kind compassion comforted her.

"I've already grieved." She did not want to talk about the loss of her baby.

BLAKE SCOOTED his stool closer and took both of her hands in his. Her beautifully tapered fingers were like icicles against his warm skin. "Caitlyn, grief isn't something you accomplish. It's important you give yourself time and space to feel the pain, the sorrow, even the unfairness of it all."

Her tears came then. A sob escaped her throat, and Blake jumped to his feet. Wrapping his arms around her, he soothed her while she cried against his chest. His heart swelled as she released her agony.

With gentle strokes of his thumbs, he brushed the moisture from her cheeks. He desperately wanted to kiss her. Instead, he breathed in the scent of her coconut shampoo and let the air out slowly to maintain control.

"I'm so sorry, Blake." She pulled away and got to her feet, sniffling. "I don't know where that came from." Caitlyn took a step back and swiped her fingertips over a smudge of mascara she'd left on his lab coat. "Oh, no. I messed up your doctor suit."

Smiling at her comment, he said, "It's fine. I don't mind." Blake felt bereft of her touch and yearned to draw her close again. He shoved his hands into his pockets.

She turned away from him and walked to the window, and he didn't dare follow her there.

"So, I guess that answers how I'm feeling." Her voice sounded small.

"It's understandable. Expected. And listen, don't be sorry. It is the most natural thing in the world to cry for a loss. It's healthy—as strange as that sounds, especially to you." Blake filled a paper cup with cool water and handed it to her before taking his seat. He typed a few notes in her file, giving her a few minutes to compose herself.

He sucked in a deep breath. "How is Colt handling all of this?" He asked because it might seem strange if he didn't. Though right then, all he cared about was comforting the broken heart of the woman he loved. Not only had she lost her baby, but Deputy Cooper told him she'd killed a man during a raid. How could she possibly cope with all of that at once?

"HE'S..." How *was* her husband handling the loss of their baby? "He's sad, of course. But strong."

"I heard there was a shooting?"

"A clean, justified shooting. Yes." Defensiveness rose from her belly and straightened her shoulders.

"It's still a shock—a trauma you have to deal with. Have you made an appointment with your therapist?"

Caitlyn sighed. "Not yet, but I'll will. Probably next week."

"Okay, but don't put it off." He finished typing. "I'll call the nurse in to draw your blood." He hesitated before he pushed the button, but after he did, he stood and approached her. "Caitlyn, you know if you ever need anything, anything at all—even just to talk—you can call me anytime. Day or night." He cupped her cheek in his hand, and for a second, she thought he was going to kiss her.

"I know that, Blake. Thanks. I'll be fine, though—I

promise. Now that I have Renegade back, I'll be better soon."

HE'D ALREADY DRAWN out her exam time for as long as he could without raising suspicion, and as it was, he'd have to take only a half-hour lunch. But he didn't care.

He couldn't seem to stop touching her. He brushed her cheek with his fingers. Thank God the nurse arrived, or he would have kissed her then. Everything in his body pressed him to do so. Instead, he stepped back and shook her hand like an idiot while she assured him her dog would be there for her. *Great.*

Blake stalked to his office, furious at his lack of self-control. Angry that he could not find relief for his feelings for Caitlyn. He closed his door and leaned against it, breathing slowly to lower his heart rate. His cell phone buzzed, and he glanced at the screen. Allison was calling. He sent her to voicemail.

Was he using Allison in the same way Kayla had accused him of using her? Was he only trying to numb his unrequited feelings for Caitlyn? God, the last thing he wanted to do was to hurt anyone. He cared for Allison... didn't he?

Blake yanked his gym bag from the closet and hung up his lab coat. Even though he had put himself in a time crunch, he needed to take this emotional mess out on his body. Hopefully, a hard workout would do the trick and he could make up a little time in his day by skipping his usual trip to the café for lunch. Snatching his car keys from his desk, he strode down the hallway toward the front doors.

Caitlyn was leaving at the same time. *Damn.*

"Headed to the gym?"

He raised his bag in answer. "My lunch-time constitutional."

He held the door for her, and when they stepped outside, the fresh air pinkened her cheeks. "Good for you." She put on her sunglasses. "I need to get back at it myself."

"Caitlyn, please, give yourself some time to heal."

She touched his arm and heat blossomed under her fingers. "Blake, thanks for caring. For being such a good friend." She slid her hand up his arm and drew him into a hug.

He dropped his bag to return the embrace and went to kiss her cheek, but at the same time she turned to kiss his, and their lips met awkwardly in the middle. Blake's arms tightened, but Caitlyn pushed away.

She apologized, "Oh! Sorry about that."

He forced a smile, though he could hardly breathe. "No worries. Call me in a couple of days. Let me know how you're doing. Okay?"

"I will." She crossed her arms around herself. "Blake?"

"Yes?" Stepping close, he smiled feeling his dimples cut into his cheeks.

"Is everything... I mean, are we good?"

"Of course, why do you ask?" His breath went shallow, and his gut tightened.

"I don't know. You're kind of acting... different, I guess.

I know you're worried about me, but I'm going to be fine. I promise."

"I am concerned for you, but not worried. You're the strongest person I know. I just want you to take care of yourself." He carefully didn't address that she pointed out his behavior. He needed to get some space—some clarity—so he backed away. "Well, I better get going."

"Have a good workout. Talk to you soon." She waved. "Oh, and have fun in Jackson Hole!"

35

Caitlyn planned to meet Colt and Jace at the ranch after her appointment, but she wanted to go home and get Renegade first. On the way to her car, she noticed she had a message on her phone. It was from a man called Jeff Dutton, a deputy marshal from the US Marshal's SOG unit, asking her to return his call. Why was a guy from the special operations group calling her?

She clicked the fob to unlock her Explorer, and when she rounded the hood, she saw Allison sitting in the car next to hers. Caitlyn raised her hand in greeting, and Allison lowered her window.

"Hi. I'm surprised to see you here."

"I bet." Allison clipped her words.

Caitlyn never knew which Allison she'd find when they met. If she wanted something, Allison could be friendly, but otherwise, she was a snipe. For Jace's sake, Caitlyn forced herself to be civil. It wouldn't do for Colt's son to be made to pay for any conflict that might arise between them.

"Have an appointment?"

"Yes."

"Well, I'm on my way to meet Colt and Jace out at the ranch. I guess we'll see you tomorrow when we drop him off."

"Yes, see you then." Flames shot from her eyes, and Caitlyn couldn't imagine what she was furious about this time.

She and Allison would never be friends, but Caitlyn thought they had come to a decent working relationship. Then there were days like this, when for no reason at all, Allison treated her as a mortal enemy. Caitlyn shrugged and climbed into her Explorer.

As she pulled up to the cabin she and Colt shared with Renegade—and sometimes Jace—her phone rang. Dirk Sterling's dark, broodingly handsome features stared her down from the screen.

She swiped to answer. "Hey Sterling. What's up?"

"Well, for one thing, I'm a little pissed that I had to hear you were in a car accident and that Renegade was stolen through the grapevine."

"Sorry. Everything happened pretty fast. I didn't call anyone."

"And that Ren won the top dog at the National Police K9 Trials. That's a frickin' big deal, Reed."

"Yeah," she chuckled. When had she last laughed? It

felt foreign, but good. "It *is* a big deal. He was outstanding, Dirk. I wish you could have been there."

"That's okay. I've seen him in real life, and that's even more impressive. I'll never forget how he saved my ass at the racetrack when he flew from the balcony and took out Anthony Trova."

"Yeah, that was spectacular, I have to admit. So, tell me. What's new up in Montana?"

"Still breaking Hank in."

"How's that going?"

"I'll deny it if you tell him, but he's turning out to be a terrific partner. He's got some twenty-something and new marriage issues, but he'll figure it out."

"And your new boss? How's she fitting in?"

Dirk paused before answering. "Emory? She's... so here's the thing. We're seeing each other."

Caitlyn laughed again. Talking to Dirk was good for her. "Why does that not surprise me? I'm dying to hear how that happened."

"Don't judge me, Reed. You married your boss, as I recall."

"Okay, that's true. But he's not my boss anymore." Though the way Colt was acting lately, he clearly thought he was. Her unsettled anger at her husband flared again, but she pushed it away. "Speaking of the grapevine. I heard your last collar escaped from prison."

"I can't tell you how furious I am about that. But I'll find him again, and when I do, I'll take him to prison myself."

"No doubt."

"Listen, beyond checking in with you, I'm calling to

tell you I recommended you and Renegade for SOG. I told a guy I know there about Renegade's success at the trials, and your record speaks for itself."

"Yeah. I got a message from him earlier. I wondered why he was calling me."

"It'd be a great opportunity for you."

"I know. A dream come true, if I'm being honest. But I have more than just myself to consider. A position with SOG would mean moving or being gone all the time."

"Maybe. You might be able to work something out. Their tactical unit usually only deploys in high-risk situations like national emergencies or natural disasters. It'd be perfect if you could be on call from Wyoming. But whatever you decide. Just thought I'd give you the heads up. I know they'd love to have you."

"Thanks, Dirk. I mean it."

"Anytime. And by the way, I heard about…"

"Yeah. It sucks, but we move on. Right?"

"It's not that easy, kiddo. I know. You need to take care of yourself. Okay? How's Colt holding up?"

"We're fine," she snapped. She hadn't been home for forty-eight hours and she was already sick of people asking how she and Colt were.

"I can see that." His softened tone told her that Dirk saw through her anger and into her pain. "Let's grab a beer sometime soon. Or even better, let's reschedule our shooting range practice."

"Absolutely." She kept her voice bright, desperate to appear as though she was holding it all together. "Can't wait to drink the beer you're gonna owe me when I outshoot you."

"Yeah, yeah. We'll see about that. Talk is cheap. I'll call again in a day or two to set something up." Dirk ended the call.

When Caitlyn opened the door to her cabin, Renegade tried to launch himself at her, but fell. "Whoa, buddy." She reached down to calm his anxiety. "You are supposed to lie still. You're okay. I'm home." Her dog licked her hands and face frantically. "We're going to get through this together, Ren. You're safe, bud. I'm here."

They sat huddled against each other on the floor and Caitlyn stroked his head and body until his breath slowed. When Renegade calmed down, she loaded him into the K9 Explorer and drove to Reed Ranch.

36

The glow of a welcoming flame blazed from the firepit in the backyard of the ranch house and when she pulled up, it warmed Caitlyn's sense of belonging. Home. This is where she'd heal. Hopefully, Renegade would find peace here too. She looked out the windshield at her family, everyone was there besides Logan, who was in Denver, and her mom, who was probably in the kitchen getting dinner ready. Her family sat on lawn chairs around the fire, drinking beer, laughing, and telling jokes. Except Jace, who sat on the ground with Dylan and McKenzie's dogs. For a moment she rested her gaze on Colt, appreciating the way the firelight played against the strong angles of his face.

Caitlyn helped Ren out of the back, and he hobbled toward Athena, Ember, and Larry. There was a fourth dog with them, and when Caitlyn saw him, her gut hardened to stone.

"Renegade, *kemne!*" Her sweet dog turned on a paw and limped back to her. He sat on her left. "*Zustan.*" She told him to stay while she stepped forward to protect him. Raising her voice, she asked, "Why is Storm out of his kennel? I don't want Renegade to have to deal with him right now. He's had enough dogfighting and trauma." Her voice cracked with emotion, which only served to make her angrier.

Jace responded first. He flung an arm around the gray pit bull. "Storm's a good dog, Caitlyn. He was only bad because the man who owned him was mean. Look—he's nice, now!" Storm slopped the boy's face with a juicy lick.

McKenzie rose from her chair and raising her hands, took a step toward her. "Caitlyn, Doctor Moore asked me to keep the dog at my kennel and watch him for aggression, which he has not shown at all. Jace has bonded with him, and he's been the perfect dog since he's been here. I promise, I would never put Jace or Renegade, or any of my dogs, in a situation I believed was dangerous."

"Dad said I might be able to keep him at your house!" Jace's eyes brightened with the statement.

Caitlyn's jaw dropped, and she stared at Colt, her brows crunching together. "Are you kidding me?" Feeling oddly out of place and more than slightly betrayed, Caitlyn took in her family as they regarded her with faltering smiles. They had no idea what she and Renegade were still dealing with. "I'm sorry, Jace, but I can't ask Renegade to share his home with a dog who might attack him at any moment."

Jace's smile fell into a frown, and he glanced at his dad. Colt held up a calming hand. "I said *maybe*. Let's just see how they do, Catie. I think you might be surprised."

Caitlyn blinked rapidly to keep any idiotic tears from

forming. Her head swam and she felt as though she were floating outside of the scene. It seemed like her husband and best friend were choosing Jace and some strange dog over her and Renegade. She knew the thought was imma-ture—even ridiculous—but with all she'd been through over the past few days, and now with everyone prodding and asking questions, it was all too much. Both she and Renegade were trying to heal mentally and physically, and right then her emotions were strong and volatile.

"It might not matter, anyway." She cleared her throat to rid her voice of the growing ache. "Ren and I have an opportunity to take a position with the US Marshals SOG Unit." Colt stood at her announcement. "If I accept, it will mean we'll be gone—a lot."

Hurt and anger flashed in Colt's eyes. "Don't you think you might want to discuss this with me?"

"You mean like we discussed getting another dog?" A wave of nausea nearly brought her to her knees.

"Catie, you and I have a lot to talk about. But as far as Storm goes, no decisions have been made. I told Jace it would all depend on how you felt about it, and if Storm and Ren got along."

Caitlyn turned her gaze to McKenzie. "Is this what you were trying to hide from me today at the café?"

"What do you mean?" McKenzie flushed when she answered, and she wrapped her arms around her middle.

"What is it you're not telling me? You kept Athena's pregnancy from me, and I can tell there is something else. I feel as though I'm not being included in my own family." Her gaze panned back to Colt who looked away. There was definitely an elephant standing in the yard, only she didn't know what it was. Maybe her skewed perception was because of the concussion, but she always trusted her gut. Her carefully constructed walls trembled, and she stook a shaky breath, terrified she was going to break apart any second.

Dylan unfolded a chair and sat it next to him. "Caitlyn, why don't you sit down? I'll get you a beer."

Colt's phone buzzed, and he sighed as he answered. "What is it, Allison? Now's not really a good time."

As he listened, his brow dipped and then his jaw hardened. His eyes shot hazel darts at Caitlyn. He turned his back to her and covered his open ear, mumbling something she couldn't hear. He jammed the phone into his pocket and when he faced her his chest and shoulders were heaving.

Caitlyn ignored her brother's offer of a seat. She needed to get out of this Twilight Zone. Confused, she stumbled toward the house swallowing a desperate desire to run from the intense feelings threatening to consume her.

She itched to call Jeff Dutton at SOG and immediately accept any full-time position he offered. If she left Moose Creek, it would solve all their problems. The pit bull could move in with Colt and Jace, and McKenzie could keep her secrets to herself, and everyone would leave her and Renegade alone.

Realizing she wasn't thinking rationally, she dropped her gaze to the toes of her boots. Renegade sensed something was wrong. He whined and licked her hand. Hormones had her emotions skittering out of control all over the place. Rather than over-react, she took several big breaths and let them out slowly. "Ren and I are going inside to see if Mom needs any help with dinner."

As the kitchen door closed behind her, Caitlyn heard Colt's angry voice. "Damn it, Dylan. I knew something like this would happen." Heavy footsteps ran across the grass and followed her into the house. Colt grabbed her arm and pulled her around to face him. "Caitlyn, what the hell is going on between you and Blake Kennedy?"

37

Caitlyn stared at him like she had never seen him before. His anger turned to fear in a flash as he watched her brow knit together and her eyes glaze over. She crumpled to the floor before he could catch her. He fell to his knees beside her. "Catie!"

Stella screamed, "Call Blake!" as she ran around the counter and knelt next to him. Caitlyn's mother lifted his wife's hand and squeezed.

Colt brushed long strands of hair out of Caitlyn's face. "Catie? Can you hear me?"

Stella grunted at his lack of action. She pushed herself to her feet and hurried to the door. "Dylan, Caitlyn collapsed! Call Blake, right away." She dashed to the sink and returned to her daughter with a cool cloth in hand. Back on her knees, Stella pressed the towel against Caitlyn's forehead. "Caitlyn? Sweetheart?"

Dylan blasted through the kitchen door, yelling into his phone. John was on his heels, pushing his way through. McKenzie followed them inside with Jace, and she wrapped her arms around the boy as if she could protect him from whatever was happening.

Colt's heart constricted. He'd caused this by accusing Caitlyn of something he knew she'd never do. And worse, he'd let her run around bashing in doors and getting into a physical altercation with a man twice her size. He had blamed her for running off, but he'd been so intent on the raid that he hadn't noticed she was gone. He knew she had been suffering from headaches, but rather than fight with her, he let her put herself in harm's way.

Colt scooped Caitlyn into his arms and stood. "Let's get her into bed." Not waiting for anyone's opinion, he carried his wife through the swinging door into the great room and up the sweeping stairs to the bedroom she'd slept in as a girl. Stella hurried after him and rushed into the room to turn down the bed. She pulled Caitlyn's boots off before Colt tucked the blankets around her. He readjusted the cool cloth to cover her forehead as the rest of the family filed into Caitlyn's room.

Dylan placed a hand on Colt's shoulder. "Blake said he'd be here in twenty minutes. Probably fifteen if he's driving his Porsche."

Colt knew Dylan was trying to relieve his tension with gentle humor, but the last man on earth Colt wanted to see right now was Blake Kennedy. It turned his stomach knowing that the bastard was the one person Caitlyn needed, so he kept his thoughts to himself.

"Catie? Catie, wake up," Colt begged as he stroked her bruised face.

Stella brought another washcloth and a bowl filled

with iced water. She took the cloth heated by Caitlyn's fevered brow and replaced it with the fresh one.

McKenzie stammered, "I thought she was acting strange. She wasn't making much sense."

"She was making perfect sense," Colt murmured. "We just weren't listening. You and Dylan—and me too, by de facto, *are* hiding something from her. She's an investigator. Did we really think she wouldn't figure it out? Then I accused her—" his voice broke.

Dylan squeezed Colt's shoulder. "Who were you talking to on the phone before all this happened?"

"Allison." Colt swallowed.

Dylan nodded to McKenzie, who took his cue, and steered Jace out of the room. When they were gone, Dylan asked, "What did she have to say?"

"Nothing I should have listened to. She's always trying to cause trouble."

Tires skidded to a stop on the gravel in the front drive. Seconds later, footsteps sounded, running up the stairs. Blake burst into the room. "What happened?" He rushed to Caitlyn's bed.

Colt couldn't look at him, so Stella told the story.

"Excuse me, Colt," Blake said. "I'd like to examine Caitlyn. I'll be just a moment."

Reluctantly, Colt stood and stepped out of the way. But when Blake sat on the bed next to Caitlyn and touched her face, it was all Colt could do not jerk him away from her.

"Caitlyn? Can you hear me?" Blake reached into his medical bag for a tympanic thermometer. He placed it in her ear until it beeped. "Ninety-nine, point seven. Let's keep refreshing that cool cloth on her forehead, Stella. I'd like to bring her temperature down without the use of medication if we can."

With gentle movements, he lifted her eyelids one at a time and studied the reaction of her pupils to his penlight. Caitlyn groaned, and her hand moved to cover her eyes.

"Caitlyn, can you hear me? It's Blake."

"My head hurts," she whispered. "What happened?"

"You passed out. But you're in bed now, and this is where you're going to stay."

"But..." Caitlyn tried to sit up, but Blake pressed her shoulders back down.

"I'm not asking, Caitlyn. This is serious. You have been pushing yourself too hard, and now your body is demanding you take the rest it needs." He turned to Stella. "Can you please get her a glass of water, with a straw if you have one? I don't want her sitting up. And can someone please turn out the overhead light?"

Colt moved, but John, who stood by the door, beat him to it. He then switched on the small bedside table lamp.

"Where's Renegade?" Caitlyn's voice was weaker than Colt had ever heard it, and it frightened him. He was so used to her powerhouse attitude and feistiness that seeing her helpless on the bed unnerved him.

"He's right here, Catie." Colt touched her blanket covered toes. "Ren's at the foot of your bed, with his chin on the mattress. He's worried about you." Colt wanted to hold her hand, but Blake was in the way, listening to her heart with his stethoscope. "I think you spoiled him in

Phoenix, letting him sleep on the hotel bed." He hoped for a smile, but she gave him no reaction at all.

Blake took the warmed washcloth, dipped it in the cold water, and wrung it out. He returned it to Caitlyn's forehead. "Why doesn't everyone go on downstairs? Have dinner and let Caitlyn rest. I'll keep an eye on her and let you know when she wakes again."

John and Dylan turned to leave as Stella brought a glass of ice water with a straw into the room and set it on Caitlyn's nightstand. "How's she doing?"

"I'm pleased that she spoke and seemed aware of her surroundings. That's a good sign. I don't like the fever, however. And I know she has a mind of her own and doesn't always cooperate for her own good, but I don't understand what caused this. I just saw her in my office a few hours ago. She was not ready to collapse then, or I would have admitted her to the hospital."

"No. It sounds like you thought she was *just fine*. Fine enough to kiss." Colt spoke the words in a low and dangerous tone.

Blake stood and faced him. "Is that what Caitlyn told you?"

Stella stepped between the two men. "This isn't a conversation that will help anything right now. Blake, is there anything else Caitlyn needs? Anything more that I can do?"

"Why don't you both get something to eat? Then you can sit with her while she rests, if you like. It won't do her any good to have you in weakened states yourselves. I'll call you if she wakes."

Colt hated that Blake could stand before him so calm

and collected. So confident. Yet on another level, he was also relieved that Blake was there. No doctor on earth would take better care of his Catie.

"I'm not leaving her." Colt pushed past Blake and took his seat on the edge of his wife's bed.

"Okay," Blake's smooth voice shot up Colt's spine causing all the muscles in his back to tense up. "Stella, would you please send a dinner plate up for Colt?"

"Of course," Stella said, "But what about you, Blake? Aren't you hungry? I'll bring a plate for you, too. Be just one minute."

Blake sat in the leather wingback near the door. He stretched out his long legs and resting his elbows on the arms of the chair, he steepled his fingers. He watched Colt for several minutes over the tops of his fingertips as Colt held Caitlyn's hand, but he said nothing.

Colt realized he was gripping Caitlyn's fingers too tightly and eased up. Breathing out his tension, he kissed her knuckles.

Finally, Blake spoke. "Didn't the ER doctor in Phoenix give you a set of written concussion protocols to follow when Caitlyn was released from the hospital?" There was an underlying anger vibrating through his words.

"He did." How could Colt defend himself? He knew Caitlyn shouldn't be doing the things she did, but it seemed like she was handling it. And there was no stopping her, anyway. "I should have insisted."

"I'm not trying to blame you, Colt. I know how stubborn Caitlyn can be. Especially when it comes to protecting Renegade. And she's an adult. She's responsible for her own behavior. But..." He let the rest of whatever he was going to say die in his throat when Stella came into the room carrying a tray.

"Here we go, boys. Chicken and dumplings. One of Caitlyn's favorites. I saved her a bowl, just in case—" She set the tray down hard on the dresser as tears flowed down her cheeks. She pulled the skirt of her apron up to cover her face.

Blake jumped to his feet and put his arms around her while she cried. "She's going to be okay, Stella. She just needs rest and absolutely no more stress."

"It's just that Caitlyn's always been so tough. She had to be to keep up with her brothers, you know. And to see her collapse like that—well, it scared me to death." She patted Blake's arm. "Thank you for coming. You are a calming influence. Just what this house needs right now."

Stella's words grated on Colt's already agitated nerves. He felt anything but calm with Blake swooping in to save the day.

Blake squeezed Stella's shoulder. "I'm glad Dylan called me. There's nowhere I'd rather be."

Caitlyn shifted, turned her head and winced. Colt held her hand to his lips, and Blake moved to his side. Bending around Colt, he lifted the cloth and turned it to the cooler side. "Caitlyn?"

Her eyes blinked open at his voice, and she studied his face. "Blake?" Her gaze moved to Colt and her brows drew together. "Colt? What is going on?"

THE END

. . .

Thank you for reading TRIALS! Ride along on Caitlyn and Renegade's next adventure in Book 8 in the Tin Star Series!

Order SPEC OPS K9 Today!

Please take a few minutes to rate and review TRIALS. Thank you!

SPEC OPS K9
Tin Star K9 Series - Book 8

A US Marshal Thriller

In this heart-pounding saga, Caitlyn Reed and her fearless K9 partner, Renegade, are handpicked by the US Deputy Marshal Special Operations Group. Their mission: to join the ranks of the most elite forces and tackle the deadliest threats facing the nation. For Caitlyn, it's not just a career opportunity; it's a chance to escape the anguish of her personal turmoil back in Moose Creek.

But as Caitlyn grapples with grief, her husband, Sheriff Colt Branson, harbors suspicions about her relationship with the town doctor, Blake Kennedy. With emotions running high, doubts fester, and trust hangs by a thread. Will Caitlyn's past with Blake jeopardize everything?

As Caitlyn undergoes grueling assessments with the USMS SOG unit, she's thrust into a high-stakes battle against a ruthless drug smuggling operation. From the treacherous US/Mexican border to the wilds of Montana, Caitlyn and Renegade must unleash their unparalleled skills to dismantle the criminal empire flooding the nation with lethal narcotics.

In a race against time, Caitlyn must summon unwavering focus and strength to confront the drug kingpins threatening to tear her nation apart. But as the pressure mounts, will her shattered heart betray her, leaving her vulnerable to the merciless grip of the cartel?

SPEC OPS K9 is a pulse-pounding thriller of courage, betrayal, and the ultimate test of resilience in the face of danger.

ALSO BY JODI BURNETT

For more books by Jodi Burnett

Go to Jodi-Burnett.com

Flint River Series

Run For The Hills

Hidden In The Hills

Danger In The Hills

A Flint River Christmas (Free Epilogue)

A Flint River Cookbook (Free Book)

FBI-K9 Thriller Series

Baxter K9 Hero (Free Prequel)

Avenging Adam

Body Count

Concealed Cargo

Mile High Mayhem

Tin Star K9 Series

RENEGADE

MAVERICK

CARNIVAL (Novella)

MARSHAL

JUSTICE

BLOODLINE

TRIFECTA

QUALIFIED (Novella)

TRIALS

-

US Marshal Dirk Sterling Trilogy

FORGED (Free Prequel)

EXTRACTION

CORRUPTION

REDEMPTION

ACKNOWLEDGMENTS

First, I must say this book was a challenge for me, though I love the story. I wrote Trials during a move from the Colorado plains to the Rocky Mountains. The move slowed me down and I had many starts and stops. And, the truth is, you would not be reading this book if it weren't for my super amazing Alpha and Beta Reading Teams!! I sent them the un-edited manuscript at the eleventh hour, and they all stepped up to help bring you the polished version of Trials. I want to give a special shout out to Chris, Emily, Sarah, Jenni, Sheila, Brooke, Marc, and David. You guys are the absolute greatest!!

My alpha reader, G. K. Brady, is a romance author friend of mine who reads my words before anyone else, and she took time away from her much needed and well-deserved vacation to read, comment, and help me wrestle this story into submission. I owe her a huge debt of gratitude! Thank you, Kae!

Dear reader – if you like to read romance, be sure to check her out her fantastic books on Amazon!

I have the privilege of writing because of the love and support of my wonderful family and friends. Thank you for your patience and care. As always, my greatest thanks go to my sweet husband who is my sounding board and sanity. He is grounds me when I need it and encourages me to fly as well. I love you so very much!!

ABOUT THE AUTHOR

Jodi Burnett is a Colorado native and a mountain girl at heart. She loves writing Mystery and Suspense Thrillers from her mountain home in the Colorado Rockies where she dotes on her dogs and horses, complains about her cows, and writes to create a home for her imaginings. She is the author of both novels and novellas over four series: The Flint River Series, FBI K9 Thrillers, Tin Star K9, and the US Marshal Thrillers. Her books are available in paperback, eBook, and audiobook formats. Inspired by nature and fascinating humans, Jodi fosters her creative side by writing, painting watercolors, quilting, crafting stained-glass, and traveling. She is a member of Novelists, Inc. and Sisters In Crime.